Intracultural Language Exchange Series

.

Meditation

as a Way of Seeing Beyond Mega Machine

by Peter Bowman

ISBN-13: 978-0692797785
(Intracultural Language Exchange Series)
ISBN-10: 0692797785

Little Man Publishing
Chicago, IL
www.littlemanpublishing.com

for my brother.

TABLE OF CONTENTS

.

CHAPTER 1
the Stadium

My toes splayed in my boots as I stirred awake. I was back in the stadium seats of the lecture hall. These days I could slip into daydreams with ease, and they were vivid, but I had trouble locating myself when I came to.

Paulie sat next to me, not taking notes, but not daydreaming either. I think his leg shook too much to doze off. He twirled his pen between his fingers and gave my side an elbow when he saw that I'd come to. I straightened up a little, widened my eyes and flared my nostrils for his amusement.

"You're missing the good stuff," he said in a dry voice. But I wasn't missing it, I was listening intently and I had been even before I snapped back into place.

Paulie and I would get a sandwich and few beers at the Campus Pub after class, mostly to talk about the movie we were about to make, "The Rise and Fall of a Mustache," but also just to drink. I could talk to Paulie; I could be myself. He said I should be Guy, in the movie, that is, instead of trying to find someone who fit the part and could grow a nice stache. I said I'd only be *Guy* in the movie if he played Guy's sidekick and nemesis *Chuck*, but I was already cultivating my stache anyway.

The movie required me to slap Paulie in the face several times. Sometimes they were more like open-hand punches. That was not the first time I had tested

Paulie's patience, but he was good with me and didn't hit me back, although I could see in his face that he wanted to. I was glad we had class together.

The class was called *Sacred Drama: Astrological Meditations*. The short round man on the stage below talked about the energies that James Merrill channeled to write his 500-page poem, *The Changing Light at Sandover*, which the class discussed in depth, on multiple literary levels, and without me or Paulie. I never read the book. I admit I just loved to listen to that man talk and explain things and read passages to us in his half-lisped, sultry voice. On occasion he'd start out of nowhere on the sacred ecstasies of tantric sex, which was fun for Paulie and me in the back of class, such a sultry voice coming from such a homely little man.

Someone told me that he'd adapted Vonnegut's *Slaughterhouse Five* into a screenplay. It received multiple awards back in the 'seventies. I sometimes felt like I was the man in that book, jumping through different moments in my life, in and out of time. I'd always wanted to adapt that book into a movie. But it had already been done, and further, it'd been done by my film professor.

He took my movie, I thought, *what a shit!* Coincidentally, this was about the time when I started to get angry. Not because he took my movie, but for reasons less defined.

The Sultry Professor had gravity to him though, the movie was just one more compelling reason to allow myself to daydream in his class, allow myself to be taken by his meditative voice. Not that I had much of a choice. The problem was that he made these cassettes for us to meditate to at home. He put his own voice on them, probably recorded in his study at home. I came to associate his voice with my sleep-like meditations.

He had us meditate on different parts of our minds, drawn from our astrological aspects He sent us across the river to a brownstone bookstore in Harvard Square. I had my planetary aspects charted, the exact position of the stars and planets at the time of my birth. I also bought a book on Astrology in order to identify each aspect and to categorize it. It didn't matter if I believed in Astrology or not. It was an exercise to get to know myself better.

For each astrological aspect, my chart provided its location in the sky, and the book provided an appropriate label according to that location. The label was made up of three categories, a *Who* of a *What People* in a *What Land.* That was one character; I was made up of eleven, apparently decided by the relationship between the stars and the when and the where I was born.

[I am with aim to repair past errors and embark on fresh experiments.]

Who?	*Of what People?*	*In what land?*
the Witch	of the Olympians	in the Entrance Hall
the Healer	of the Masters	**in the Hospital**
the Hero	**of the Charmers**	in the Everyday World

So, I had one, *the Witch of the Charmers in the Hospital.* This was called homework, not so bad, better than reading the 500-page poem. I pulled ten more characters out, and each week, I was supposed to meditate on one. But this is when I found myself at an impasse, voices dog-piling in my head.

The first time I closed the door to my room and sat on the floor. I put my headphones on, just in case my roommate was listening. He had graduated the year before and now sold real estate, which made me uncomfortable. The dramatic, slightly-lisped, Sultry voice came in. He talked slow, calm, and he asked me to sit comfortably and close my eyes. I closed my eyes. He told me to picture myself in a chair at the edge of a chasm, wind blowing on my face, sun at my back.

Picture a window in front of you in the air. He told me that a guide would come and take me through the window, and I should let myself be taken –said in a sultry voice. Paulie would be losing his shit right about now... *shake it off! Just relax and go where your guide takes you.*

I did as he said, and I poked around in my head for fifteen minutes. I focused on *the Witch of the Charmers in the Hospital,* but I wasn't entirely sure how I would keep my focus on her. My mind had a tendency to wander.

The progression started slow: chasm, chair, guide, window, then to the house in which I was born, the Harvey house, the back yard, steadily moving backward, the back door, the mudroom, the playroom, the circus, and then flash and flood.

When I opened my eyes, I cursed the tape and the Sultry Professor for making me dive back so deep. I was crying. Why was I crying? For no reason really. I held stuff in sometimes and with my guard down, I guess my body just let it out. That was not what I expected. I didn't like it, and it wore me out too. I went to bed and slept the whole night. I didn't dream of anything, just black.

The next week I tried to listen to the tape again, but only because I needed some points for this class, and that poem, what the hell were they talking about? If it was such a great piece of literature then how come my dad had never heard of it: ex-Jesuit priest, theologian, scholar. If I wanted to read dense books that I couldn't understand, then I'd read Marcus Aurelius or some Seneca. I sure as hell wasn't about to read a 500-page poem that was supposedly channeled through a Ouija board.

So, *the Muse of the Stars in the World of Childhood* was the next character on my list.

My roommate had thrown a party the night before, and I was still a little hung over. I had convinced him to invest in some super8 film to shoot at the party and to make a video of the event. The film was expensive, from a company in California which cut 16mm in half to fit into a super8 camera, allowing for faster speed film than normal (which means I could shoot in low light). But the night was a bust, nothing worth shooting, and I never asked him for his half of the money. Instead, I just closed the door to my room.

I started the tape and the Sultry voice got me as far as the beach and eating strawberries, then a gazebo, but that's when I stopped it. That voice was starting to get to me. It kind of creeped me out. The last time I "meditated" it hit me like a tooth cleaning, left me achy. I felt like I needed more control; I couldn't let down my guard like that, let myself go places I couldn't un-go. At the time, I valued my ability to be un-gone.

I just sat in silence with my big headphones on. I didn't want to think about my hangover; I really wanted to keep my focus on the task at hand, the meditations. I started to think about *the World of Childhood*: playing 'guns', shooting bullets from my mouth, snow hills and forts, snowballs and cars, underneath the neighbor's porch, cat piss and beat up old porn mags, riding bikes and stealing cakes from the cakewalk, feeling sinister. It was not hard to stay focused on this character, just good fun. Then I opened my eyes when I felt like it, and I wasn't crying at all, but I was still tired afterward. I wrote down everything I saw, Chapter 2 in my journal, like I did the last time, like I was supposed to.

The next week was the last time I meditated though. I talked to Paulie in class, and he wasn't doing the meditations. I couldn't shake the tired from the past two attempts, and I spent half the day sleepwalking and half the night dreaming of black. The meditating required so much slowing down, and I was so busy with my movie and other people's movies.

I did the sound for a film about a woman's

self-esteem, and gaffing for one about the perfect cup of coffee. I was the assistant director for my friend Anna's film about an angel on a bus. And my digital editing class pulled me in like a vice. Now that was real meditation(!), hours and hours in front of a glowing computer, fingers chopping and clicking and plucking moments out of the aether. The immediacy was very satisfying. Meanwhile, the Sultry Professor was reading a poem that never ended.

This last time, I didn't even think of using the tape, I just put on my earmuff headphones, sat on the floor and closed my eyes. I thought about *the Hero of the Curious in the Everyday World* part of me. But I didn't start of the edge of the chasm. I just started. Things were less defined, and I felt that was okay.

This time I saw images of my brother Henry. I thought about how much we look alike and how he could be my twin, except the timing wasn't right, he was born two years before me. What did I do for those two years? Did I wait patiently inside my mother? Chapter 3 became a story about my brother.

I saw him as a young, scruffy kid who always had dirt on his face. I saw when he started to get clean, around high school. Clean cut, clean shaven, but then the childhood dirt returned. I saw him become a weed-hungry hippie.

Played his own songs at an open mic at Gloria Bean's coffee shop. Played with his devil sticks in the park. Wore his ferret like an accessory around his shirtless neck and shoulders.

His ferret was Wyatt, like the gunslinger Wyatt Earp. My mother hated Wyatt. She didn't want that smelly rodent anywhere in the house. So my brother made an cage for him in the yard. That worked for the Fall, but when Winter came, it got really cold, like most Chicago winters. My mom made him bring the little guy inside. Compassion, then play. Then love and loyalty.

Wyatt was every quirky rebellious ounce that Henry was. And it frustrated my mother to no end, until the day she embraced it. I think she loved him just like he was a little part of Henry. Finally, she could take him in her arms and rock him to sleep. Not since he was a toddler and even then, a hefty task with the restless Henry, wild crabby difficult troubled disobedient intense Henry.

More flashes of my brother. Played guitar with him. Threw a party with him when my parents went out of town. Smoked a hitter behind the garage. Then I gave him a hug: the young scruffy, the clean cut, the hippie. And I ran back through the field, and a toucan told me to climb a tree and start a bicycle shop with my brother.

I'd never told a story about my brother before. It was refreshing to let it come out of me, but it was exhausting again. I hadn't thought about him in awhile; he'd moved out West before I left for school.

I didn't want to meditate anymore! This class took up too much of my time, and the Sultry Professor started talking about dolphins as aliens and Feminine Trines all pulled from the cosmos by a seyoncing gay couple in a castle, and I wasn't sure if he was still using metaphor or not.

He taught my film comedy class too (he was tenured). He would use the class session to do hacked-up comedy routines instead of teaching. He had a fan club amongst the grad students and a few hipster undergrads, and they ate it up, fawned over him. He also married a former student of his; she now taught screenwriting, pregnant with his child. I sat in the back and didn't laugh. I hated the fact that he'd opened up a door in me. I hated that I was attracted to him. I hated his gravity.

He was very attentive and concerned in the one class, very serious about us finding all the different parts of our selves, while in the other he was rehashing old comedy bits from Woody Allen and Peter Sellers. Did he not recognize me in the back of class? Did he not remember talking me into a hypnotic trance, swimming me through the dark recesses of my mind, burning me out? He left me in the back seat of the car, a child lulled to the sleep by the nostalgic ride through the countryside, and I woke up alone, strapped to my child-seat in the dark vacuum of the garage. I needed this class, for the credit, but also because I held things in. I had things that I needed to get off my chest.

Fuck it! I'd go it alone. I didn't need to meditate. I knew these people, I could fill up the rest of the journal myself, Chapter 4, Chapter 5, Chapter 6. I caught glimpses of them throughout the day and late at night and when I first woke up. I would write them down, sketch them in my notebook, Chapter 7, Chapter 8. Part of me took care of me, helped me cheat my way through the semester. I could rely on me, and I would not turn on me and do impressions of old comic deities.

I would teach myself how to get the stories out that needed to come out. I was no longer dreaming of black anyway. I woke in the middle of the night, having just been pulled from the most lucid dreams, and I was bringing back halfs of irrational systems led by tangled dynamics and intersecting timelines, Chapter 9, Chapter 10. They would congregate in my reflections as I muttered my way through the semester.

The Dreamer of the Olympians in the Shadow World followed me to digital editing. *The Philosopher of the Daydreamers in the Everyday World* helped distract me just enough to survive my lectures. I ate lunch with *the Fool of the Uncanny in the World of Intimate Others*, just me and him. I watched scrambled out smut films with *the Old Person of the Greatests in the Playground* on the cable channel we didn't get. *The Warrior of the Masters in the Spotlight* and *the Heroine of the Nobilities in the Danger Zone* tried repeatedly to save *the Sacrificial Victim of the Earthy People in the Entrance Hall* (we called him *SV of the EP*), but *SV of the EP* was my drinking buddy. He was in the entrance hall of every bar, and let's face it, there was no saving him.

But even with all of these chapters coming out of me, when I woke in the middle of the night, I would wake to the dark vacuum of the garage, abandoned, strapped to my child-seat. I just kept telling myself stories to keep me company. Some I told to myself on the train, some I told to myself in class, but mostly I told them to myself in my sleep. Those were much more engaging. I'd wake up and try to remember them, but they disappeared faster than I could ever retell them, only scraps remained, like bruises. I was losing control.

CHAPTER 2
the Witch of the Charmers in the Hospital

I got one down, straight from a dream. It wasn't like the rest; it hovered patiently, waiting for me to piece it together and put it to page. It was comprehensive and concise and articulate, and I found it addicting. I could read it over and over. I felt like I opened the pores in my brain so wide that it just snatched this story up, right out of nowhere. It was seven o'clock in the morning by the time I finished getting it down, then I slept 'til the late afternoon.

I took the train with Mary, who was not one of the characters in my head, and who could talk and talk in a very natural way. I always felt that I lacked an ease about myself in that way. When some people get nervous or stressed they find more of themselves, like Mary. (I tended to go the way of isolation.)

What she said reminded me of something I heard while sleeping in class. Maybe it wasn't what she said, but rather the fact that she kept talking after I was done listening. I thought about how stories are told to you even when you're not listening, and this happens with the stories that you tell yourself too.

The Sultry Professor had explained when he was on a tear: the story of the sacred drama (distinguished from profane drama through the existence of revelation and mystery and the on-going) contains memory and dream that penetrate the story led by the feminine...

One   → unity and direction
Two   → duality ←
Three   Δ the liminal trine
(A triangle, the mathematical symbol for change!)
1. ♂ masculine   2. ♀ feminine   3. ⚥ the synthesis of.

      He read it off the board, chalk-smeared hands: the masculine, imbibed with the force of singularity, joined with the feminine, of dialectic potency, to synthesize in sacred drama. With metamorphosis as the central action/metaphor of the sacred. Metaphor connects the planes, and verifies.

      It Verifies! I wish you could hear him talk. I had to sit in the back because I would sometimes well up (and because I didn't want to get called on).

      "It verifies," I told Mary. Mary didn't hate the Sultry Professor, she just hated all the grippers, his fan club. She smiled, and she was looking at my mustache. I was getting self-conscious, but the train pulled up to our stop, and she didn't comment on either. We got off the train and walked to the Communications building which housed the editing suites. We each went to our separates suites. I edited a fake movie trailer for my digital editing class, five hours of meditation, computer glowing, fingers chopping and clicking and plucking moments out of the aether.

      It was unconscious. So my head went to the story, but it was more like a play, and my mustache was now tingling.

      I caught the last train home by myself and I was still coming down from the buzz of editing. Mary had a night class, and she popped in around dinner time to say 'bye, which prompted the first intermission. I walked out with her to get a few tacos-to-go, then went back to editing. I was now feeling the rumbling of cheap tacos and soda liters in my stomach as the street-level green line trucked itself back up the center of Commonwealth Ave.

The story came out as a play, and I hated plays. I don't know why it came out as a play. I always fell asleep during them. My mother made me go to all of my sisters' high school plays, and they were slow (intermissioned) torture, even if my sisters were very talented. Somewhere inside me I supposed I may have had an affinity for plays, but I did not believe this story came from me.

The first order of business was to get to the bottom of this. So, when I got home I went right to sleep. And that's where *you* came in.

You were sure someone inside me knew something about this, knew something about theatrics. Even when you were little, you always went to Ajua first. Ajua checked with Nobody, but neither of them had heard anything. You thought it might be *the Dreamer of the Olympians in the Shadow World* (Chapter 4). He said it wasn't him, but suggested *the Philosopher of the Daydreamers in the Everyday World* (Chapter 5, you think, you seem to have lost track). He liked your question and thought about it for awhile, but never got back to you. *The Fool* was a fool. *The Old Person*, addicted to scrambled porn. *SV of the EP* felt badly for not having produced it, but you gave him a break, he'd been having a rough go of things.

You asked some of the woman closest to you, but *the Heroine of the Nobilities in the Danger Zone* had no time for metaphor, no time for any of this cloud-headed bullshit. She explained that there are real problems that people faced, set in reality. Pretty righteous for a woman who herself had been revealed through metaphor only a month before. You think she was still upset with your relationship with *the Sacrificial Victim*, a relationship she once called perpetual.

Then, you were back to the first aspect, *the Witch of the Charmers in the Hospital*. You went to talk to her, in the hospital. You were hoping she worked there, but as it turned out, they'd checked her in a long time ago. Fortunately, it was visiting hours. And you've been trying to be more present in your life, so you start with the present tense.

You kneel by her bedside, and you know her infections are getting worse. They're eating away at the stump where her leg used to be. You think you might catch something, but she holds your hand, and you forget all about it. You don't know what to say to her. She's got no teeth, and her hair isn't up in curls like usual. There are no formalities; she's too close to death. You play with the ring on her finger and the watch on her wrist as she stares off at the wall.

Then she tells you the watch was given to her by your mother. You tell her that she reminds you of your mother. She smiles at this, but you think she thinks you're someone else. Then she stares off again. It's hard for her to feign any kind of interest. There's truth in that, you think.

And what about the story you keep hearing over and over in your mind? You ask her.

Have you heard the story? (Although, it's more like a play.)

No, she says, but that's all.

Did it come from you, grandma? You don't know why you call her grandma. She turns to you and puts her hand over yours.

I am but part of you, she says.

Yes, but did it come from the part of me that's you?

She's shaking her head, becoming more awake, more attentive. *Tell it to me*, she says.

Okay... You suppose you could do that.

Tell me what you've heard, she says and moves closer to the side of the bed. She looks at you, eyes clearing by the moment. She winds her watch and waits patiently for you to begin.

I don't really know where to begin.

Where did it begin for you?

You search for an answer...

Well, how does it make you feel?, she asks.

You let out a sigh, *I feel relieved, like it allows me to set something down, to be less angry.*

Start with the anger, she says, *start with the*

daemon anger.

But, grandma... Why do you keep calling her grandma?!

One, two, three, eleven, she says, *tell me about eleven.*

You know she's referring to the missing aspect, the one with whom you've not yet met. You were supposed to have meditated on eleven, but you only did ten because you didn't read the directions properly. *I feel I should give it an introduction.*

No, she says, *just tell it to me slowly, and ee-nun-see-ate.* So you wet your lips and begin to set the stage once more.

It takes you several nights to show her what you mean. She continually asks for you to start over, so you do. The first night you kneel by her bedside, the second there is a chair for you, the third night she props herself up with pillows against the bed board and touches your face twice, and the fourth night you wheel her around the grounds in her wheelchair. When you finish, she asks you to tell it again and you do, because it's as if you are being read to, like when your dad used to read to you and your brother.

You watched your dad laugh beside himself. He read about the Laputans of Gulliver's Travels, who would get so lost in the inebriation of mathematical contemplation that they needed to employ servants to smack them in the head and bring them back to sobriety, just to make it through the day. Like that, you walk attentively next to yourself as you usher her through the garden of the hospital, telling the story of Leaf getting lost in the inebriation of his own mathematical contemplation, as he divides himself and divides himself once more.

But when you finish, you ask her again, *Do you know this story?* She just smiles and looks off, her eyes are glazed, and she's sunk into herself. She goes somewhere you can't go, so you wheel her back to her room. You lift her back into bed, and she's so light. There is very little to her: so low in the flesh, so high in the bone, going places you can't go.

When you come back to visit the next night, she's dead.

So, you revive her, which you can do, and you prop her up against her pillow, and she smiles and is happy and says, *it's nice to see you.* She asks you to tell her more, and when you finish, you finish with the nap that Leaf lays into, and the Queen Lizard filling the entire sky with her smile, again.

Her eyes begin to glaze and her skin droops, *And what happens next?*, she asks with a flat smile. You look at her and open your mouth, but you don't know what else to tell her. *Then the sky was filled with the Queen Lizard's smile.* When she realizes that's all you have, she winds down like a clock, ticking slower and slower, falling further and further out of sync with the rest of the world.

You revive her again, which you can do, and she plays the same scene over like a recording on an answering machine, and you hear the symphony strings slowly coming in.

Peter, it is nice to see you. I'm delighted that you've come back to visit. Please tell me more. Why is she calling you Peter? You can't tell her the same story again after that kind of response, after she's died on you. You just say the last line, *the Queen Lizard's smile fills the sky*, but you say it like a question.

And what happens next?, she asks with the same flat smile. You don't open your mouth, just chew the inside of your cheek.

Please, just answer the question, why won't she just tell you where the story comes from? Your jaw aches from the tension. Why won't she just tell you? The way she talks makes it sound like you should know the rest, like it comes from you. But it doesn't, it was told to you like a play, and then you told it to her.

You thought maybe it came from the *aether*, that it was divine; you were thinking maybe it was channeled like James Merrill channeled that 500-page poem. But she's implying that it came from you.

That means you don't know yourself very well. That means the distance between you is too big to see, that one of you is beyond the horizon while the other is here beside you and you've never met that you over there and you've never seen that you, but that you has the same raw nerve endings and tenses just like you, and that you is part of you. You were thinking maybe you'd been blessed, but you realize that you just hid things from yourself.

You revive her again and before she can say

anything, you kiss her forehead, which you can do, and she stops at *Peter*... She smacks her toothless mouth like a cow and her cud. She looks through you and asks, *what happens next?*. Remember thinking how you start to cry, remember how your head gets heavy, and you let it lay on her lap, and she rubs your back. Remember you don't know if she dies again because you fall asleep. And when you awake, you're in your room, and you wonder if she carried you back to bed and did she think? *so low in the flesh, so high in the bone.*

You feel ashamed and awkward and you won't visit her for a long time. You won't visit any of them. You let parts of you take care of yourself: you give up control. You ignore the rest of you, until your brother comes back to town.

CHAPTER 3
no deeper a sleeper

I popped two pills before my screen comedy class. These were cold and cough pills, and I did have a cold and cough, but I popped them purely for recreation. Now I had an excuse to sit in the back and not laugh, not let him engage me.

Walking from the train, I thought I heard my phone ring in my coat pocket, but I pretended not to. I knew that even if my phone had rung it would be Alex, and I had nothing to say to him that couldn't wait till after the pills had kicked in and the class had ended. Alex was making a movie with a big production value, and I was helping him, but I didn't want to talk to him now. Besides, I'd have felt even more stupid if I snuck a peek, and my phone hadn't rung. I'd have felt like people would've known and would've laughed to themselves at me for my self-consciousness and my vanity.

I could have imagined the ringing though, like I imagined people calling my name on the street. Not imagined, like daydreamed about how nice it would be if people would call out my name, but imagined like I'd hear my name, but Nobody called it (Peeeete! Peeeeter!). Sometimes it'd be faint, could have been a squeak from the train, sometimes it'd be clear, and eee-nun-see-ated.

"PETE!" A yell from a not too far distance, as if they were trying to get my attention. I'd turn to look and see no familiar faces, only looking at me now because I was looking at them. Then they'd know that I'd turned and looked to a voice in my head, and people would laugh to themselves at me for looking, and believing.

Five minutes after class began, I was really feeling the pill slug kick in. It dragged on the frenetic conversations exchanged across the small room, leaving a congealed trail of echoes. These were conversations involving the Sultry Professor, but not class related, just his "comedy" bits, which he'd stolen and delivered in affected casual conversation. The fawning and laughing would begin, but I had my slug. It wore a little shell that protected me from the barrage of nervous energy spewing from the affirmation-hungry fanclub. It barked: *Don't bring that shit around me! Fucking relax...*

always bringing that shit around with them, carrying it with them like a bad smell they don't even know they have, it clings to the air and they're steeped in it, and if I hang around long enough, it'd saturate my skin and before long, I'd mistake it for a natural smell, but that shit isn't natural, it's a manufactured by-product of impiety, a deviation from everything graceful...

I hid in my silence, unnoticed, apathetic. I treated this class as a test of endurance. I am who I am; they are who they are. And the pills had engulfed my entire brain. I am a slug.

[I   -   am   -   a   -   sluuugg!]

Three hours of slug reminded me why I didn't

like drugs for recreation. But that was the same regret I always felt, just part of the cycle. I met Alex and Mary in the editing room. Alex was excited and anxious. He'd left a message on my phone asking why I wasn't picking up when he could see me walking from across the street. Maybe he tried to call my name too as I tried to pretend I didn't believe in voices coming out from my insides.

The footage looked very nice, very clean, but my slug lacked enthusiasm, and Alex was annoyed. He went to class and left Mary to digitize the rest of the footage.

Hi, Mary.

Hi, Pete.

You look tired.

Pete, you don't even know, I'm exhausted.

You should go to sleep, Mary.

She hadn't had more than a few hours of sleep per night in more than a week, but she's got work, work, work, even though she spent the majority of her time worrying about her work and not doing her work.

Go to sleep, Mary.

I know, I know, shit, I should, I just have to digitize, and then write a paper for my Hitchcock class, and I have to retake a psyche quiz or she's gonna fail me.

You're gonna fail?, I asked.

Well, no, but I'll definitely get a C and I can't get a C right now.

Go to sleep, Mary.

She pushed back from the computer table and hugged me around my waist, and I thought maybe she was going to go to sleep with her head against my chest.

I hugged her back: she was short, and it was easy. I could have gone to sleep myself.

But out of nowhere came a giddiness, a sort of mania. It was nice to see her smile, but she was talking faster than I could blink, running circles around my slug. I had to leave, but she came out with me to get a snack. The crisp air outside bought me time, and I walked to the convenience store with her.

Right by the gummy worms, she told me a one-sentence story that was over before it began, and all I could think was to count the *ands* and *buts* and *becauses* to see if it really was one sentence. Then I let her know that she just told me a one-sentence story. She got a little embarrassed, but went on again. She had an energy only nerves could produce, manic nerves. And I knew she was a trembling engine just before breakdown when I saw her vibrant smile sputter into trepidation the moment I left her to catch the train, a hollow moment when she no longer had anyone to receive. She was alone, she would have to slow down, and it wouldn't be long before the blurred stress that she sped by came into focus.

As for me, my slug would eventually drag me to sleep. I would continue to hear Nobody call out my name on the street. And I would wake up to people bombarding me with bullshit and think it just a natural smell. Until then, I had my dreams. I lied to myself and said those too were divine, sacred, given to me from above instead of told to me from a me I didn't know.

But I wasn't me in my dreams, I was you. Here's an example of my dreams of you.

The Deer Killer Dream

first, Guy starts to take things out on you
but you're not the man you were 15 years ago
and Chuck had just given you a small white
mouse to hold and care for
so you tell Guy you'll beat his ass
and you do
then you're in the park with your mother father
your brother and Meta
Meta tells you how lonely she is
there is a father teaching his two sons karate,
actually smoking a pipe while his older son
teaches his younger son,
Meta starts to help teach the younger son
she's pretty good
the older comes and talks to you and your
mom and dad
but he talks mostly about rifle positions
for shooting deer
he wows you all with his ability to recite
complicated and intricate positions,
but scares you in his comfort with killing
to the point of despair and holding back tears,
but you're able to ask him how many deer
he's killed and if he has a license
he says he works with a delay and your mom
concurs that when she hunted she would use
a delay also, perfectly legal

but you're disturbed and you have to leave
on the conveyor belts
a passage too narrow, so you're stuck
it's fine, you just shouldn't have done that
your mom helps you out with some scolding
but it was worth a try
but it wasn't, because the impressionable youth
does the same, he's chubby and he gets
caught way before you,
you yell at him at first
that's what happens when you kill deer
but then you realize that he can't breathe
and he's dying, so you try to pull him out, but
you can't from where you're standing,
so your mom
pulls him out and he's alright,
but you're too overwhelmed
this time to hold back your tears,
even on the crowded
public transit and you huddle in a corner seat
and whimpering sounds escape even though
you try to let them not, and there's a man
seated right next to you,
but you can't hold back anymore,
your mom comes over to console you,
babe in arm, but you're inconsolable,
even when you wake up.

"Are you awake back there?"

I admit to daydreaming, but not like in high school when all I daydreamed about were the breasts of the girl one seat ahead of me in the next row over. I didn't think about sex much these days; I had so many mathematical problems going on. Paulie nudged my leg with his own.

"Me or...?" Paulie said as he pointed to me.

"No, you. What's your name?"

"uh...me? I'm sorry, I'm Peter."

"Yes, Peter, well, tell us what Merrill means when he talks about the duality of bats?" The whole class looked back at me. I hovered over them all in the back row of the stadium seating: the fanclub, the grads and the undergrads, the innocents, the guilty, the Sultry Professor. I had the attention of the entire room, pedestaled. I straightened myself up in my seat.

"I didn't get a chance to do the reading last night."

"Well, that's too bad. Do the reading! Anybody else?" A few giggles from the fanclub, and that was it.

He didn't even know my fucking name! I'm in two of his classes, small classes, twenty, twenty-five people at the most, and he didn't even know my name. Caught me at my most apathetic, when I wanted to stand and yell back in my loudest stage voice, "You changed my life! I respect you to no end! I'm with you, I get it, no one has ever made more sense! You're blowing my fucking mind back here! SLAUGHTER HOUSE FIVE!!!!!"

I didn't get a beer with Paulie that day. I walked up Commonwealth Ave. back to my bed. Four trains passed me by.

We talked about it, me and you, and you and Ajua, and Ajua and Nobody, and *the Sacrificial Victim* (*SV of the EP*), but it was no use. *Do you know what happens next?*

I don't know, I've tried. *SV of the EP* really wanted to help, I could see the frustration mounting on his face. But his fate was inevitable, he was marked for the sacrifice. It was a part of his name, for Christ's Sake, *the Sacrificial Victim of the Earthy People in the Entrance Hall,* a constant reminder that he was the first one to go, to be given up, and it was hard for him to focus on anyone but himself. But that was alright, he was busy dealing with his own things.

That was around the time when I ran out of money, none in my pocket, none in my bank account. I got in line at the grocery store with bread and peanut butter and jelly to hold me over until my parents came for graduation a week later. And I wasn't exactly graduating, but I was gonna walk anyway.

My credit card was declined, *fuckin' loser*, but again, he took the bullet for me. I heard the echo of the gunshot that put him down once more. I don't know who started calling him *SV of the EP*, it was just better.

Nobody and Ajua played word games and you mostly talked to pigeons, so that was nice, but we were helpless. You wanted more too, more than anyone.

Dream for Exam Day

Look over the city of Greece
where you always hang out, see
the water, go down the
steps careful not to get
wet, see the brand new cars,

cross the water but you're
scared. The fountain is
Extravagant!

Your parents have a baby (chubby).
"That baby's fat," you say.
Baby holds your hand, says
the most beautiful, funny,
witty, amazing things to
you. You laugh hysterically,
so hard, you cry.

Your parents are very happy
that you've been touched,
you laugh so hard that tears
burst out of you. Pour out of
you. You are so happy to be
blessed with the attention
and wisdom
of such a baby (chubby).

Mary got a big plate of wings that we split. She had slept all afternoon and was back to her old self. She seemed receptive, so I told her my story, the one that was like a play, and Mary listened intently as she dipped her wings and chomped her celery and blue cheese. She had an uncanny insight into me, so I thought she might understand where it came from.

She said she understood it. *Glory be!*, I was ecstatic. But she didn't know why she understood it. It just made her feel good. It was nice to know that someone else understood it, even if she didn't know why. I think it made her cry too, although not in front of me. We could wring a pocket of all its thread with the tension that mounted from the things we shared so intensely but could not quite capture in conversation. She tried to explain it, but the only thing we could settle on was God, or some form of God, some kind of divinity. That didn't explain anything.

She asked me if I ever thought a baby was so cute that I wanted to eat it, just bite into its soft little head like a peach. It was then that I wasn't sure if we were talking about the same thing. I did not crave to eat a baby's head like she did. Yet there were fantastically incongruent desires that I also had, and I knew that she wouldn't actually eat a child's head, or I was pretty sure. We didn't have to be exactly the same to understand each other. And we didn't have to be different to not.

She laughed at herself, but she was not apologetic.

She would always shamelessly described these intense feelings to me, which were obvious anomalies. She described them as if they were everybody's everyday... *Wait, Stop!* I think that's where we switched places, me and you. You were always better with her.

The strings come in and that signals the entrance of Peter, but there are horns too, which means that the Wolf is not far behind, and where are the rolling drums of the Hunter? Where are the rolling drums?

I may not be able to aptly describe her or conjure her memory and that makes me a little sad. I don't believe I was entirely present. From inside me, *the Philosopher of the Daydreamers in the Everyday World* (was it Chapter 5?) wanted me to add that she wasn't my girlfriend, and a week after we graduated, she got a boyfriend, and I moved back to Chicago. He thought that there was a hole in me from that. I thought there was already a hole in me. He conceded, but maybe she was plugging it up, or helping to, and now it was bigger. I said he might be right. In Chicago, my heart beat so fast sometimes, and *SV of the EP* became my best friend.

CHAPTER 4
the story that's more like a play

[The lights dim and the stage clears. Figures in black shift around the furniture and set dressings, preparing for the coming scene. On the stage's wing, a spotlight reveals a wall for puppets or marionettes, curtains drawn. Then lit from within and dark all around, now a stage within a stage.]

[An oboe sounds, the same oboe that signaled the entrance of the Duck in the symphonic telling of Peter and the Wolf, but no Duck appears. Then the bassoons for the grandfather and his warning, but no grandfather. Humming strings, chopping violins, plucking cellos, but no Peter. There is only the sun going down on a grammar school classroom, and the blinking afternoon hours hovering above the heads of underused, thoughtful children.]

Wednesday is Exam Day; the Committee takes day out of the day for the exam.

Exam Day happens every single Wednesday. But this Wednesday is special because the Mill is up running, turning, cranking and creating. Dr. Soloman finished on Saturday, rested on Sunday, and when Monday morning rolled around, he pulled the switch. And the Mill was up running, turning, cranking and creating.

"Creating what?" asked Henry, who always sat in the front row, but always to the very left. Henry could only hear out of his right ear. Leaf would always sit behind Henry, and he whispered in Henry's deaf ear, "Black Electricity."

"Why, Black Electricity," said Mr. Foot. Mr. Foot wrote it on the chalk board, "Black Eee-Lect-Triss-Sit-Tee. Can you say that, students?"

The class repeated, "Black Eee-Lect-Triss-Sit-Tee." All except for Henry and Leaf. Henry was looking out the window at the giant smoke stacks of the Mill, while Leaf tried to turn invisible with his Invisible Glasses, but he doesn't know how to use them yet.

"Now, remember, students," Mr. Foot cooed, "Tomorrow is Exam Day, so we won't be having any day. We'll continue on Thursday with the numbers 9, 10, and my favorite number 11."

Leaf walked behind Henry on their way home from school. They walked past the Stadium. They swam through the Running River. They climbed across the roof of the Glow Home.

"What is Black Electricity?" asked Henry, who always peeks through the first window of the Glow Home to watch the Queen Lizard's daughter dance, and to listen to her sing. Henry could only see out of his left eye, so he would have to alternate between seeing the Queen Lizard's daughter dance, and listening to her sing.

"Dr. Soloman," whispered Leaf into Henry's deaf ear. Henry listened for the Queen Lizard's daughter's song on the roof of the Glow Home, and at the same time was looking at the giant smoke stacks of the Mill.

The day was Tuesday, the day after Dr. Soloman

had pulled the switch. Dr. Soloman stared into the depths of the furious fire which always burned the dictation of the Committee from the Wednesday before, after the Committee commits the contents of the dictation to memory. But this Wednesday was going to be special because the Mill was up running, turning, cranking and creating Black Electricity.

"It is better if I show you," said Dr. Soloman. Dr. Soloman scratched his long beard, the long beard that he can't cut, but only keeps growing and growing. "I will show you tomorrow."

"But isn't tomorrow Exam Day?" asked Henry.

"Exam Day," Leaf whispered in Henry's deaf ear.

"Yes, tomorrow is Exam Day," said Dr. Soloman.

In the morning on any other day, the sun comes up and the Glow Home dims. The sun taps Leaf on the shoulder, and Leaf awakens. Leaf taps Henry on the shoulder and whispers in his deaf ear, and Henry awakens just like that, on any other day. But the day is Wednesday.

On Wednesday the sun doesn't come up and the Glow Home never dims. On Wednesday the Committee takes day out of the day for the exam. And they examine for the entire day while Leaf and Henry and all the other students play with the Queen Lizard and the Queen Lizard's daughters.

Leaf flies behind Henry, and Henry flies up into the air to the top of the Stadium. They run over the

Running River. They land on the roof of the Glow Home, where Henry dances with the Queen Lizard's daughter, and Leaf sings the most wonderful songs to them. Also, Leaf turns invisible with his Invisible Glasses, without even trying, and this is how every other Wednesday has gone. And like every other Wednesday, Leaf and Henry weren't awoken by the sun.

Dr. Soloman tapped Leaf on the shoulder, and Leaf awoke. Leaf tapped Henry on the shoulder and whispered in his deaf ear, and Henry awoke just like that, like never before. For the first time, Leaf and Henry were able to see the glow of the Glow Home in all its brilliance, on the day without day, Exam Day.

[This is the first intermission and the end of Act 1. The lights go down as the figures in black shift around the furniture and set dressings on the stage within the stage. These figures are much smaller because the stage is smaller. A small french horn plays slow and steady, like the Wolf prowling the meadow from the edge of the forest, but there is no Wolf, not even a small one. There is only the light of miniature street lamps, casting the big shadows of Leaf, Henry, and Dr Soloman as they walk through the empty streets toward the Glow Home.]

Henry peeked into the first window on the roof of the Glow Home, but he didn't see anyone.

"But why are we here?" asked Henry, who up until now was free from his plague of curiosity, but only because he thought he was still dreaming. Henry tugged on the tips of his wings. Henry always brings his wings to the Glow Home, just in case the Queen Lizard's daughter wants to fly with him, but the Queen Lizard's daughter was not there, and Henry was not dreaming.

"The Mill," whispered Leaf into Henry's deaf ear. Leaf shivered in his boots as the cold reality of the west swept across the back of his neck. Leaf didn't bring his wings. He left them next to his Invisible Glasses, hanging on a hook under the desk with locked drawers.

"The Heart of the Mill," said Dr. Soloman in a weakened state. Dr. Soloman had not slept for years, ever since the Committee commissioned him to build the Mill, and he took his first sip of Meta Nectar, the nectar which he stopped taking the day he pulled the switch so he could, at last, slip away into a peaceful sleep. The effects of the withdrawal were beginning to set in, and the good doctor was not going to put up a fight.

Dr. Soloman opened up a door in the wall of the Glow Home. He slid the panel behind the door aside. Beyond the panel was the Heart of the Mill, not a human heart, or even a baboon heart, not a heart like any animal, but the heart of a machine, an institution, a heart not unlike the heart of the Committee.

Henry peered through the door, beyond the panel, right into the Heart of the Mill. Then Henry turned his head and listened, but he didn't hear a heart. Henry heard the soft sighs of mistrust, the drone of a world uncovered, the spinning motor of a dream displaced.

Leaf tried to whisper a warning into Henry's deaf

ear, "Come back, Henry. Come back," but it was too late, and the truth ran through Henry like the ripple of a rock in a puddle, but like the ripple of a rock that turned the puddle to stone, and for a lasting moment, Henry turned to stone.

Dr. Soloman unsheathed his harmonica and began to play, a rousing tune, a tune that once brought the Queen Lizard back from a frightful spell, back before the dawn of the Queen Lizard's daughter, when the Queen Lizard was still vulnerable to the influence of the Committee. Henry's skin began to crack and shed like glass to the roof of the Glow Home. Leaf shut the panel to the Heart of the Mill, and closed the door that covered the panel, and Henry was able to move his lips and furrow his brow.

The tune, however, had roused more than the diving spirit of Henry, and a patrolling Orb, out on his beat, caught wind of it. Before the Orb blew his circuits at the tingly, incomputable softness of the tune, he transmitted a distress signal back to the Committee, interrupting the examination on this very special Wednesday.

The pillars began to shake, the roof began to tilt, the ground beneath them began to rumble, and the heavens cried out for the uncertain future of a boy who shed his skin. Henry and Leaf rolled toward the edge of the roof. They were able to climb down to safety, but Dr. Soloman, in his weakened state, was lost in the crumbling debris, and his sweet tune sank to a void.

A most wonderful woman hovered over the boys

with a cheerful grin, the same woman who played the villain in the stories that the Queen Lizard's daughter would tell to Henry and Leaf. And just like in the stories, the most wonderful woman cheerfully inquired, "What are you boys up to?"

Knowing that if she caught them she'd make them tell the truth, Henry and Leaf ran. "Don't run, you silly boys. I just want to talk to you."

Henry and Leaf ran through a neighbor's yard, but stopped at the steel gate. Strange as it may be, neither Henry nor Leaf remembered the steel gate, though they passed through the very same yard with Dr. Soloman an hour before. The red dingy bars of the gate bent like a curtain, making enough room for a small boy to squeeze through. Henry squeezed through. He turned to Leaf, but Leaf had seen the hands of the most wonderful woman take hold of the bars and bend them apart. Leaf froze in his moon boots.

But Henry didn't see, and Henry couldn't wait, for fear that the most wonderful woman would take hold of him and make him tell the truth about what he'd heard behind the door, beyond the panel on the roof of the Glow Home. Henry turned to go, and he was too far away to hear Leaf whisper a warning.

The most wonderful woman, with her cheerful smile, hovered over Leaf once more. Leaf ran back the way he came. He ran past the Glow Home, through the rough foliage, and into the Rope Fields. The most wonderful woman rushed to prevent him from crossing the border to the forbidden land, but she was too late, and Leaf was miles away.

[This intermission is much shorter, so that the story does not loose the momentum of its emotionally-charged second act. The lights dim one last time as the small figures in black clear the stage for the third and final act, while the music plays on. The strings swell, the winds blow this way and that, and the rolling drums weave in and out, and if there were Hunters they wouldn't know what they were hunting, but their guns would be loaded and ready to fire. The frantic heartbeat and quick breaths, ground coming up to meet galloping feet, all slowing to skittish fatigue, then wary approach.]

Leaf wandered the Rope Fields for most of the night. He was tired, but he could not have been more awake. He was lonely, but he was with two of himself. He was scared; they all were scared.

They came across an enormous topless tree. Floating from the tree was a rope ladder. At the base of the tree was the Tavern of Thieves. Leaf thought of the times when he and Henry spent Wednesdays dancing and singing with the Queen Lizard's daughter, and the rope ladder, like the most wonderful woman, was a part of the stories the Queen Lizard's daughter had told them.

The Queen Lizard's Daughter had said, in her raspy scary-story voice, "At the top of the floating rope ladder there are no rungs, but you must continue climbing or you will fall past the roots of the Topless

Tree to the hungry Soulmongers below." Like any story, there were exaggerations and metaphors, and Leaf saw the Soulmongers were nothing more than aged students, cast out into the Rope Fields long ago, lacking the courage to climb the rope ladder, but eager to take whatever they could from the wounded, those who hoped and tried, but fell.

"Are you gonna climb it?" asked Seraph, the larger of himself. Seraph had messy hair, and a twitch. Daniel, the younger of himself, stood beside Seraph, observing him. Leaf whispered that he wasn't sure if he knew how, but Seraph didn't hear him.

"I'm gonna climb it," said Seraph, "You're damn right I'm gonna climb it." Leaf whispered that he didn't think it was a good idea, that there was only one way to climb it. Daniel messed up his hair and began to twitch, just like Seraph. Seraph watched a boy fall from the ladder and watched his soul get eaten below, and so did Daniel.

"Weak bastards. I'll do it. I'll climb the stinkin' ladder," said Seraph.

"Weak bastards," muttered Daniel.

"Not weak, I don't know... a little maybe, I mean, I guess," whispered Leaf, who was developing a twitch of his own. After Seraph, he was the next up the ladder, followed closely by Daniel.

The journey up the ladder was no simple task. The wind blew strong up high, and the rope burned Leaf's hands. A falcon mistook Daniel for his lunch and flew away with him. Seraph feared that Leaf would pass him, so he broke off a branch and cast it down. The branch poked Leaf in his right eye, blinding him. The temperature dropped as Leaf ascended, and the hearing in his left ear faded to a void. If not for the warm blood dripping from his eye to his ear, Leaf would certainly have lost the hearing in his right ear as well.

Seraph reached the last rung on the ladder. Leaf waited to see what he would do. Seraph continued to climb, commanding the rungs to exist. He climbed to the top of the last rung, and on his next step, he reached but grasped nothing and fell all the way down past the roots of the topless tree.

Leaf watched as the Soulmongers swarmed around the fallen Seraph, spilling out of the Tavern of Thieves, eating every last piece of his soul. He thought of his Invisible Glasses, and how he wished Seraph could wear them now.

Now a third of himself, Leaf reached the last rung of the floating rope ladder. The two ends of the ropes floated somewhere up at the top of the topless tree, and as the Queen Lizard's daughter told, lead straight to the door to the House of the Sidhe. Then she would no longer speak in her raspy scary-story voice, but in the most beautiful, funny, witty, sincere voice that would sometimes bring Leaf to tears, although he'd never admit it to Henry.

And what ever happened to his best friend in the world? Leaf closed his one good eye and remembered his best friend in the world. He remembered how they would always fly to the top of the stadium, and his inquisitive nature. He remembered that although Henry never heard what Leaf whispered, he always knew what he was saying. He remembered not being able to warn Henry about the red dingy bars, not having the voice for it. He remembered how he used to sing the most wonderful songs as Henry and the Queen Lizard's daughter would dance.

Leaf began to hum the tune to his favorite of those wonderful songs. He imagined he was wearing his pair of wings, and a weight was lifted from his bony little shoulders. He began to float up towards the top of the topless tree. Leaf sang loud. He sang about how he wished Henry had never looked into the Heart of the Mill, never asked about Black Electricity.

When Leaf opened his good eye, he was waist deep in branches, the tops of branches, and he could see farther than he'd ever imagined, past the Rope Fields, past the stinkin' empire of the Committee. He could see millions of beautiful, funny, witty, sincere voices of the Queen Lizard's daughters. The sun began to peak around, letting in the first few puppies of day, then spilling out a hound dog of morning light.

Leaf floated down from the top of the topless tree, and snuggled comfortably into his bed, just for a little nap. There he meets Henry at the top of the stadium and together they fly to the roof of the Glow Home, where the Queen Lizard's daughter waits to go swim in the fountain. And the Queen Lizard's smile fills the entire sky.

[The play is over. The curtains close, then open so that each can take a bow to a few scattered applause. The little actors all join hands and bow together, and the orchestra plays them out.

You stir awake because you'd fallen asleep somewhere in the second act. The house lights come up, and the few in attendance file down the aisles and out the back, but you stay, slouched in your seat, head propped up in your hand. Your lids are heavy and reluctant, so you close them once more and fade to black.]

CHAPTER 5
the Talking and the Running

My brother moved back from Oregon where he spent five years after being out of high school two. I insisted he move in with me in a four-bedroom in Wicker Park, where I lived with friends from high school, sort of a flop house. People coming and going, sleeping on couches, always someone to drink with. He slept on the enclosed, unheated back porch in the dead of winter, but he was happy to. He'd spent a winter in Oregon in the abandoned conductor's office in an old train yard, so the porch was fine.

I was just happy to have someone around that really knew me and understood me. Everyone hanging around was concerned about the night life, the city bars and who was going to be there. I did too. I found a balance between working little enough to allow enough time to hang out, and working just enough to pay for it. I worked by myself as a house painter, a Friendly Painter, in fact.

The Friendly Painters began as an expression of two entrepreneurs, me and Josh. Our motto was *Friendly Painters: we'll paint the shit out of your house.* And we did for a while. C-way joined us, and we landed our first big job: a huge three-story, multi-color Victorian. We finished the job in 3 weeks, walked away with a fair amount of change in our pockets, and we held our heads high. A week later, lightning struck the attic and the house burned up. Our motto after that was *Friendly Painters: we've only lost one house to fire.*

I think everyone was disenchanted. A few more small jobs, then a big one, a brand new house on the north side, we were fired after two weeks. Apparently new houses are a different beast, and we were in over our heads, slow and fumbling. Then my cousin's house way out in burbs... C-way had started his own College Pro crew, so it was just me and Josh, who grew tired of my *work-just-enough-to-get-by* mindset. So, it was just me, painting apartments in the city for my landlord, living for the 4-day weekend.

My brother was a welcomed relief. He would hang out with us at parties and bars, but also just with me. I felt much more relaxed with him around; there was no pretense. I think he was waiting for the right time.

After a couple months of getting used to each other again (we'd grown up so much since we last lived together), he told me that he'd talked about it with his ex-girlfriend one time, about the guilt he felt for not being a good brother, for not protecting me like he should have. I brushed it off at first, as if I could make it go away. I told him, you don't have to feel guilty for anything. I was just happy to see him now and to live with him again, not since we were kids. Then he asked me if I was okay.

I don't know. He just didn't know if anyone had ever asked me that before. My mother tried once in high school, but at the time I was so far from that me that I closed her down by getting crabby, like she was annoying me. No one else ever had, somewhere they knew that I would close them down too. But Henry didn't care. He wouldn't be closed down. He was immune to my crabbiness; he invented it, I think I learned it from him. I tried to say that I was okay, that it used to bother me but it didn't anymore, but I couldn't hold back my tears. They just came like they always did, when I was fine.

He told me that he was sorry that he allowed it to happen. He was sorry that it did happen. That it wasn't my fault. I couldn't hold back my tears still. I just cried, and he hugged me, and we smoked a cigarette, and we talked about it, which was something I needed badly. He said when I went into seventh grade, I became too cool for him. I smiled because I knew it was true, but secretly I still looked up to him. He said he didn't know that. Then we talked about it some more, which was something I needed badly.

I'd meant to talk about it. I had rehearsed the story in my head so many times before. I knew the power in talking about it, the release. But the only person I'd ever talked about my secret with was myself. I thought that was enough, but there are parts of me that won't even talk to me, so all that needed to be said was never said. Somehow, I am not enough for myself. Imagine that. I need people. I need people in my life that I'm honest with. I need to feel connected to people and trusted by people. I need to trust people.

Not long after, I told everyone in my family what had happened to me. They knew, but I told them anyway. I talked to each of them about it, I talked to all of them about it. I talked to groups of them about it. I talked at dinner, I talked on the phone, I talked on long walks. I told people who didn't know, I told my friends, I talked to a therapist, I talked the shit out of it with my girlfriend, poor gal. I didn't want that secret anymore, I talked and talked about it until I was so sick of talking about it, and then I would sleep.

I talked about it with you while I slept. Of course, it wasn't the kind of talking that one does while awake, much more fat and saturated, much less in focus. I think something my brother had said flipped a switch. So, you said you would run back to the beginning.

You run to the Hospital, straight to hospice care where you know she'll be, but *the Witch* was already taken to the morgue. This time, you're too late to catch her. You press the down button on the elevator, and press it and press it, but you're impatient, and you burst down the stairwell. The steps move too fast for your feet so you slide down the railings with your hands, then jump down the shaft in the middle. And you're falling. You drop for what seems to be like forever, you know that you can't revive her this time, that it's been too long.

Your grandmother died this summer, and your grandfather died too, six hours later. Both in comas in separate rooms of their house because of the infections in your grandma's leg, their lips wet because their children wet them. Her breath slipped away slowly. Your mom and her sisters told your grandpa, and he left after her, just like her.

You're falling, and you know you can't revive her this time.

So, you just remember. You remember what she asked you. *And what happens next?* And you remember what your brother and you had talked about. You grab for the handrails of the steps, sputtering to a halt. You climb back on the steps, up to the next landing, and into the hallway off the stairwell, which is long and narrow. It's dark, but there is a soft orange light shining from the first door in a long row of doors. You go to the light of the first door, but you get distracted from a dream of a different memory. Everything else disappears.

You can't remember exactly what it was, those polyhedral shapes that you saw when you had a fever as a child. You were pointing to your brother who sat on the edge of her bed, and you tried to tell her, *there's Henry*, but he wasn't really there, and your mother held you in her lap, and brushed the bangs away from your forehead.

You did see him though, and you saw those slowly spinning shapes when he was gone, and when she left you alone in her bedroom with just the soft orange light and the heating pad, you reached to hold them, and they disintegrated between your thumb and finger like an ice cube under running water. You felt the tingle of the ice as it melted, pockets that hollowed and left spiny edges which crackled as they got thinner and thinner.

But you felt it in your whole brain.

It was a joy. And that must have been where it began. Not the anger, but the loneliness. Because no one else had seen them, or felt them return. It was just you.

Now, you feel more, you know what happens next. No lights fading, no dark figures shifting set pieces, no puppet stage under dim light, and no orchestra giving symphonic warning to each character's entrance. It does not play on a stage or a screen, you walk through it. The story starts again and it's no longer Exam Day. You reach across his shoulder and shake him gently, and he wakes up.

CHAPTER 6
the Heart of the Mill

Leaf awoke from his nap. "I'm gonna burn it," he thought. It was a thought that was left over from a dream, and he didn't know exactly to what he referred, but he was not confused either. It had been seven years since the Committee was dissolved, and the people elected a Board. The Board felt no need to examine the sleeping students, Black Electricity had since been replaced with coffee (Columbia-grown), and the Heart of the Mill was now the store that sold it. Wednesday was no longer Exam Day, just a day in the middle of the week, halfway to the weekend. That part of Leaf took care of itself, as a part of him always did.

Leaf wiped the drool from his cheek and headed down the back stairs and out the door on his dirt bike. He had a bad dream, and his face relaxed from its usual scowl long enough to show fear, but waking to the shadows of his room, the scowl returned. And the bright sun made it easier to scowl, the way his eyes squinted and the middle of his brow drew to the bridge of his nose.

He rode past the stadium, where he saw kids picking up a game of football. They didn't wear any pads, just let their little bones crash and tumble to the ground. He rode past the Running River, which was now just the river. He rode past the Heart of the Mill, tables set up outside on a patio (a very nice patio!), a line out the door, and a stencil of ominous hooded Committee members on the storefront window, holding hands in a circle with a bolt of black lighting hovering above.

Had it been seven years or seven generations? They reduced to archetypes, as if only children lost in the over-activity of their imagination were ever in danger, as if all that was valued and held dear was threatened purely in a theoretical sense. They played the part of evil, the part of evil in a child's story.

And Leaf believed them to be so, his journey to the Rope Fields long since shelved away in his memory, losing his brother Henry to the clutches of the Committee, a bad dream. And the death of Dr. Soloman? Well, who the hell was Dr. Soloman? Was there ever really a doctor with a long beard which kept growing and growing?

Leaf's hearing had returned, and he could see shapes and colors with his bad eye, twenty/twenty when he wore his thick, lopsided spectacles. His mom told him it was a bad eye that he was born with, and he believed her.

Leaf rode up to the Wilson's penny store and lay his dirt bike on top of Wylie Soskin's dirt bike. He peered into the storefront window with his hands shading his eyes. His thick, lopsided spectacles clinked against the glass. Wylie gave him the middle finger, and a big smile. Leaf smiled back.

Wylie loved *Spree*, but Leaf preferred the *Bottlecaps*, chalky and sweet. Each slipped a pack into the pockets of his baggy pants and left the store buying only a 5 cent *Laffy Taffy* and a *Bazooka Joe* between them.

Wylie even stuck around a bit to talk to the cashier about the potato chip promotion posted behind the register. *You could win a canoe!* Wylie didn't want a canoe; he was only exercising his gall. Leaf was not so bold yet, and he quietly snuck out the door when he had his chance. Then they rode off to jump things.

They jumped the curb in front of Leaf's grade school. They jumped the dirt mound at the end of the playground. Leaf didn't go to school there anymore. He'd graduated from sixth grade, separated from what he'd known to go to the school in the woods. They rode up the ramp and jumped off the black top. And they were chased out by the mustachioed janitor after Wylie pissed on the side of his car.

Heart-thumping, unable to wipe the grin away, Leaf pedaled hard to the alley behind the Pilgrim Church. Wylie met him a moment later, entering from the other end. They were safe behind the Pilgrim Church, which had the ability to change into an aircraft, an underground bunker, and a jungle when necessary.

They lay their bikes down to jump over bushes. Leaf found a higher bush and jumped that. Wylie strapped on his anti-gravity sneakers, and stepped up to the challenge. The bush burned with blue, raising the stakes. Leaf smiled again, entranced by the danger as Wylie barely cleared the blue flames of the burning bush. He landed and rolled through the grass, looking back at the quivering branch that clipped his foot.

The Rope Fields returned to Leaf for only a second, and the shivers ran through him, standing his nostalgia on edge. He longed for that seriousness, for that uncertainty. *But what were the Rope Fields?*

They raised the stakes higher and higher as the sun got lower and lower, and finally, on the way home, they came up with a new handshake: a clasp of the right hands around the thumbs clapped from the left hands, and then released, all in one fluid motion. Wylie went home to an empty house, his working mom left the fixings for a Sloppy-Joe in the fridge and a 32 inch TV in the den. Leaf arrived twenty minutes late for a dinner at the giant oak oval table.

Henry was there, and so was the Meta (his little sister), his mom, and his pop. His elder three sisters were not present, two at college, Margie at rehearsal, chairs held their place. His chicken breast was a little cold, but the peas and carrots, and mashed potatoes still melted butter. He had missed grace. So, under the watchful eye of his mom, he crossed himself and muttered something unintelligible under his breath. Even so, the one-word sentence that came out seemed to lift some weight from his bony little shoulders.

Henry reached under the table and pulled out a few hairs just below the knee on Leaf's calf. Leaf slammed his hand on the table. Everyone jumped. His pop asked what the hell was wrong with him. His mom told him to eat his peas. The Meta, or Anne Marie, put her hand over her smile, and Leaf shot an accusation in the form of a glare toward Henry, who calmly ate his own peas. An explanation had always proved ineffective, so Leaf put it in his slowly filling bottle of emotions and regarded Henry as invisible for the rest of dinner, even when Henry tried to pulled out one more.

Since the incident seven years prior, his relationship with Henry had become more antagonistic. Not right away, but slowly, like the way Leaf's hearing slowly came back and his vision cleared, slowly like puberty. Leaf's time in the Rope Fields had left him distant, and Henry could do nothing but harass to be close to his younger brother, the younger brother who once followed him through the river and to the top of the stadium. Leaf couldn't help but see the world differently, including his brother. Besides, Henry would never listen anymore, and Leaf didn't feel like telling him.

A retreat up the back stairs after dinner left Leaf alone in his room once again. He lay on his back on the top bunk of the red metal bunk beds and tossed an old deflated basketball up and down. He thought about the bad dream that he'd woken up to that morning, and wasn't sure it was so bad after all. What was he all upset about anyhow? The question was rhetorical, but AJua answered.

"The woods."

"The woods? How do you know?" Leaf asked in defense, and not rhetorically.

"I asked Nobody and he says you're scared of the woods."

"You're scared of the woods!" Leaf responded with a smirk, as if exchanging insults.

AJua admitted it, "I am scared of the woods."

To which Leaf threw the ball harder, and it bounced off the ceiling and returned just as hard against his stomach. Leaf buckled and rolled off the bunk to his feet. He stumbled out the bedroom door and slammed it, leaving AJua sitting on the edge of his bed, and Nobody sitting on the edge of *his* bed.

When Leaf was younger and tailed his older brother, and he himself was tailed by his younger sister, and they would march around the house, picking up buckets and putting them on their heads and climbing from couch limb to chair limb because the floor was made of molten lava, it would sometimes rain awesome thunderstorms. The thunderstorms came as residue from the dissolve of the Committee, so they brought with them a smell of hope. To some, it was hard to smell, but Leaf could taste it clear as day.

Anne Marie would get scared. She was much too young to remember the scary stories the Queen Lizard's daughter would tell to Henry and Leaf, the ones that scared in just the right way. They scared awe into the little boys, like a roller coaster with its illusion of danger. And Pop would sometimes read them stories before bed too. While Anne Marie took a bottle to sleep, Pop read about the misadventures of Huck Finn and Tom Sawyer, and about the dark corners of Pinocchio, and the Lilliputians of Gulliver's Travels and when Gulliver was the size of a Lilliputian himself. But Anne Marie was not privy to this, and she would get scared by the thunderstorms.

Leaf would yell up towards the heavens, "AJua,

stop banging on the roof!"

And Henry would play along, "Yeah, stop all that banging, AJua!" And Anne Marie would look up at them, eyes clearing of fear and filling with interest. Then she'd look up at the roof, and back to her brothers.

"Who's Ashoowa?"

Leaf would explain: "He's my friend, and he's up there on the roof. He's upset because he's getting all wet, but Mom says he can't come in."

Henry would smile because he was proud of his little brother, and a little tickled. He would ask, "Why won't mom let him in?"

"Yeah, why can't he come in?" Anne Marie asked as well.

"Mom said he can't because he's all wet, so he has to just wait till he dries. So, we just have to tell him to stop banging on the roof." Leaf would yell, "AJua! Stop banging on the roof!"

And Anne Marie was empowered. "Yeah, Ashoowa. Stop banging on the roof!" The rain would fall, and lightning cracked the sky, and AJua would bang on the roof, and the children would yell at him at the top of their lungs to stop all that banging. Eventually, he would stop, and the rain would fade, and nobody would hear from AJua until the next time a thunderstorm came a-blowing.

Well, nobody but Leaf. AJua came to his roof more often than the rain, and Leaf would let him in. AJua would sit at the foot of Leaf's bed, and Leaf would talk to him and tell him about his day, about his mind, about the Rope Fields, about all the things he'd been saving in his bottle. And AJua would listen, and he would cry, so Leaf wouldn't have to. And when AJua would get too tired from crying, he would bring his friend Nobody with him, so Nobody would listen to Leaf as well and Nobody would cry, and Leaf and AJua didn't have to.

Leaf told AJua about the kid with the big forehead, who everyone called Forehead, who would put Leaf in a headlock during lunch at the school in the woods, and his lopsided glasses would get smushed, and he'd have to straighten them. He and Wylie had different lunches, so Leaf's waywardness left him as a target. Forehead was a good foot taller than Leaf, and Leaf had not yet developed the skills to deflect such attention.

"But why did he pick you?" AJua asked.

"I'm too nice. He needed someone to put in a headlock so he would look more useful to all the other kids who had nothing to do."

"So, you were doing him a favor?"

"Yeah, I felt bad for him." Leaf shrugged. "It's a curse, I'm too nice."

AJua reversed the flow of his vision and looked back into his brain, although he appeared to be looking out the window. Leaf got wary; he was never sure if Nobody was around or not. AJua returned his vision to its proper flow.

"Nobody says you were scared to stick up for yourself," AJua reported with sincerity.

"I mean, I wasn't scared. I was really calm,

except for that second when he choked me too hard, then I gagged. But when the bell rang, I told him I had to go, and he let me go."

"Nobody says you lost your voice like you used to." AJua looked at him with sympathetic eyes. "Did you lose your voice, Leaf?"

Leaf put his head on his pillow, thinking about the question. It was a good question to ask, and he appreciated Nobody's candor. But he really felt that Nobody was wrong this time: he was very calm about the whole incident, about all the incidences. AJua sang Leaf to sleep, and Nobody cried until he ran out of tears.

His brother, Henry, woke out of a sleep so deep he forgot where he lived, and more importantly, how he fit in. After clearing the crust from his eyes, his room looked familiar enough to place it, but it was still unclear as to how he was a part of it all. He started small: outside the door was a hallway to a kitchen where he would eat Cheerios and read the funnies, then out the front door he would head across the street to school, but he'd stop and have a smoke by the gym doors until after the bell had rung, and he'd be late for his first class. This much he placed, but his unsettled feeling remained intact.

He and Jen had a smoke by the gym doors as he'd foreseen, and the bell'd rung six minutes prior. They didn't talk about much, although Jen would've, she had a lot to talk about. Her mind raced in the morning. It started knowing exactly where she was and how she fit in, almost as if she never actually fell asleep.

When Henry threw down his cigarette and headed in, so did Jen. Fortunately, their first two classes were working on Mr. George's team, and they were rarely supervised. They were to build the sets for plays which were few and far between, and look busy if anyone came around, which no one ever did. And Henry was happy to be left alone, and he stopped asking questions ever since the most wonderful woman caught hold of him seven years prior and made him tell the truth about what he'd seen behind the door, beyond the panel in the heart of the mill. He'd learned too much already. He may have learned everything there was to learn.

On occasion, he still felt a surge of Black Electricity pulse over his skin, remnants of his exposure to the concentrated core that lay deep within the heart of the mill, the core that, in theory, was supposed to sustain itself forever, but only lasted as long as the Queen Lizard allowed it. The theory was oversimplified, and barred the millions of essential, seemingly negligible components that make up a dynamic system in its natural state. The burned out core remained in the Heart of the Mill, as a sculpture on a pedestal, next to the cream, sugar, and coffee cup lids.

But the occasional surge that Henry felt gave precedence to the theory that the core had merely transferred its power, leaving what was now in the coffee shop for a path of less resistance.

Henry bought coffee from there before. He

recognized it as a coffee shop first, then had a brief recollection of Dr. Soloman and the rousing tune he'd played to bring Henry back from a deep sleep, and crack the skin that had hardened around him. But a quick infusion of highly caffeinated coffee (Colombian-grown) allowed him to shake the memory and leave it next to the globular sculpture near the cream, sugar and coffee cup lids.

The last glimpse he caught of the memory was that this place was once the Glow Home, and there was a daughter that used to live here. Henry thought, *maybe above the coffee shop, I don't know.* It was hard to place, and hard to know exactly what he meant by a *Glow Home*, just like the difficulty he had when he woke up in the morning. The distance between the worlds was just too big now, it was almost impossible to bring anything back.

By lunch time he caught up with his world and now led the way. He pulled his world around wherever he went, confidently walking the halls, greeting his friends, acquaintances and security guards alike, at last, belonging.

Security guard Clem belonged there as well, making no judgment, saying hi as a matter of course, *if you know someone, you say hello.* That made it easier to watch for the smokers and the drug dealers too. He knew Henry.

Henry had found a loophole to the no-smoking-on-or-around-campus policy. By smoking in his own yard across the street from the high school, he had only to answer to his own mother, who'd he'd worn down with thick resolve and persistence. Henry often sheltered other smokers as well, giving them immunity through association, picking up stragglers here and there who were about to get busted: "Clem, he's with me."

"Then you gotta stay in the yard, Henry. You know there ain't no smoking around the school." Clem shook his head as he spoke.

"I know, I know. Stay in the yard, man," Henry barked at the straggler, who was anxious to comply. Henry's credibility lay somewhere between his ability to police those under his wing, and in the firm respectful tone he used with Clem. Henry knew he wasn't boss, but he belonged, and he knew how things worked. He may well know everything, because...

he's heard things, heard the heart of the mill, and although he may not quite remember it, he knows, he may keep it locked up inside like a relic in a church, like the cloth used to give birth to the Jesus baby, but more likely like the nail through the feet of the Jesus man that held him to that cross for fourteen hours, piercing his flesh and bone...

"Jesus, man. You're stepping all over my mom's flowers. Watch where you step, suck-ass." He tried to stay tough, but Henry let a grin seep out after successfully slipping the word suck-ass into his daily speech. Giggles, the lumbering oaf who treaded the pedals, took a step out of the garden dirt, then giggled. He took one last drag from his cigarette, then flicked it at Henry, who swatted it out of the air with his free hand, then was up and on top of the lumbering oaf before he had a chance to giggle again. He punched the sides and thighs of Giggles, who then giggled between his cries of pain.

"Suck ass!" Henry stopped the pounding with a grin and returned to his stoop to light another smoke. There was a chorus of laughter among the loiterers, and Giggles giggle faded to a nervous chuckle as he righted himself and wiped the dirt from his forearms.

"You didn't have to sodomize me." Giggles lit another smoke.

"Apparently, I did," Henry said through a long drag. He had never been told of the burning sulfur that rained down upon the cities of Sodom and Gomorrah, and he'd never been told of Lot's wife, who turned to a pillar of salt after she looked back on the burning cities when she was warned not to, but he didn't have to be told, because he already knew.

He looked past the oaf to the giant green soccer field across the street. His eyes were narrow, and they would stay that way for the rest of lunch, not saying much at all, not until he fell asleep that night, then they danced and screamed wildly in their sockets under the cover of heavy lids.

While sleeping he felt his inquisitive nature return. It was okay to ask while he was sleeping. What did he see seven years ago when he looked into the heart of the mill? What did he hear? He saw Nobody, as Leaf called him, the same Nobody who now sat at the foot of AJua's bed as AJua sat at the foot of Leaf's bed. He saw Nobody sodomized, but it wasn't until he turned his head were all of his questions answered. He did not turn his head to hear, but rather to look away, to not see. But he couldn't un-see, and he knew that too, and then he knew exactly how he fit in.

I am a coward, he thought.

Leaf woke in a fright. His heart pounded in his chest. His mouth was dry, and crusted rings of snot lined the openings to his nose. He sat up. He found his feet rubbing their soles against the mattress. The room was dark. No AJua, no Nobody. No Henry on the bunk below him, where he could just feel an empty bed. Henry always went somewhere else when he slept. Leaf knew no deeper a sleeper.

Leaf was alone, and the idea seemed to comfort him. He lay back down and pulled the covers to his chin, but continued to search the darkness with his eyes. There was a vacuum to the room, no noise, and this part of being alone, he did not like. Leaf would have preferred the emerging footsteps of the drippy basement-stairs creature to this. At least those would have been tangible, at least he could have fought back. His teeth began to grit and his temples swelled. There were no thoughts in his head but one.

It is so quiet. He said hello and it echoed through the cavernous halls of his brain. Then there was nothing. He followed the dark recesses, feeling blindly with his hands. Then he heard a faint laugh, no, two laughs. A little hope shone in the curled corners of his mouth.

Hellllooooo.

The echo returned, but Leaf realized that it was not an echo, but rather a mimic of an echo, followed by the brimming laughter again. He sped up through the halls of his brain and started to run when he saw a small light at the end of the hallway, the under crack of a door.

Who wants to swim?, Leaf screamed and the echo came back, *Hello, hello, ello.* The laughter could no longer contain itself, and burst open as Leaf dove straight through the door and into the bright, clear pool at the center of the enormous fountain. He swam up through an endless submersion with his hands outstretched in front of him. He took several gulps of water, which were also deep breaths, and his thirst and desire to be immersed were satisfied at once. The water blew through his hair and cooled his face.

AJua and Nobody each took a hand, and like a catapult, flung him through the water in the sky, and he was way above the ground, looking over the whole city and running around from roof to roof, pedaling his way to the tops with his hands. Leaf balanced on the ledge of the Queen Lizard's house and could feel the anticipation all over his skin as he knew that her daughter was just inside that room.

When he poked his head through the wall, he could feel her eyes on him. She took hold of him and brought him out onto the balcony, which may have looked over the whole world, and she hugged him. And it was then that Leaf realized that she was sad, but also afraid.

He realized that he was afraid, and he held her so tight, and she began to weep on his shoulder. She thought, *we can't all go.* And at the time he understood.

It was the hope that he was afraid of. It called to him, offered him comfort like no other, and he was deep in it. Almost too deep. She began to hum to him as they swayed back and forth on the balcony, and it was that tune that allowed him to flush out everything: all the hope, all the fear, all the worry and anxiety, all of the things that Leaf pulled in around him in order to not be alone. They flushed out from his eyes, and flushed out from his groin, they dripped from his ears, and were plucked from the tips of his toes in twos.

Leaf woke again, but the sun was peeking in the window this time, and the vacuum no longer crowded the room. He could hear the deep breaths of Henry on the bunk below. He could taste the yuck in his mouth. Things were. As they were most often early in the morning, things just were. The urine puddle drawn off from his groin *was* too, and it was getting uncomfortable. It was still early enough for him to strip his bed and hide the dirty laundry in the hamper, wash down the pee-pad, and make up his bed with fresh, clean sheets. That's exactly what Leaf did, and he'd almost forgotten all about it by breakfast. But the calm remained. Somewhere he understood, and the calm remained.

Dream that is not a dream, but a confession –
  The Nail and the Toe:

Boofu, or more likely Bu Fu, for Butt-fucked: that's what they say to you as a kid, behind an eruption of laughs. You got boofu-ed, or just boofed. At least they try to hold the laughs in, but the moment one breaks, they all break. It does sound kind of funny, but not to you.

These aren't the kids on the playground, because it's only the brothers down the street who know. You hang out with them every single day and everyone is uncomfortable with it. You are best friends with the younger, who is your same age. The older is older by a year and he does most of the sharing. He shares it with a few friends, and the friends bring it up, when it's opportune to cut you down. A good day is when you all stay distracted enough not to dwell on things in the past, maybe a small joke , but they move on. You shake it off. You're strong, no harm done. Continue on.

A bad day is when you all watch TV and are bored. You're a target, because they can sense that you're uncomfortable to begin with, a little off balance. They can smell it on you. All you need is a little push in one direction and you're flustered, frozen. You have nothing to say. You can't talk, only an occasional nervous laugh, and a weak attempt to pretend like you aren't dying inside. But you are dying, slowly and painfully.

For years this happens, until Junior High, when you get new friends, more friends, friends your own age that don't put up with the bullshit of the older neighborhood kids. Friends who don't know. You stop hanging out with the older neighborhood kids. Except the younger brother, still best friends, until high school when you drift apart. He never makes fun of you. Only gets uncomfortable and leaves the room. Who wouldn't be uncomfortable with it? You should leave too, but you stay.

Years before, the kid who lives across the alley from your family is your senior by four years. He is, by most accounts, a little monster. But he gives you yogurt that they keep frozen in a big basement freezer. He's your friend, both to you and your brother. Maybe you're four or five or six, you can't remember. You hope you're not seven, because the older you get, the harder it is to blame what happened on your age and your innocence. Really, you don't know why you allowed it. You know it's bad. You know the whole thing is bad.

The kid across the alley and your brother and you are in his room. He has the playmobile pirate ship, which is the biggest toy you've ever seen. You never have toys that big.

He wants to play *truth or dare*. He dares you to lie on your stomach on the bed with your pants down, so you do. Your brother continues to play with the pirate ship. The kid from across the alley lies down on top of you and put his penis against your butt. He doesn't move around, just lies there. You lie there too, all his weight pressing against you. You lie there and watch your brother play with the pirate ship. This is you being molested.

When he hears his dad coming up the stairs, he gets off of you, but pants are still being buttoned when the door opens, so his dad breaks you all up, sends your brother and you home. He calls your dad, and your dad calls you both into your room to talk about it. You sit in a circle, gathering to talk about something very important.

He asks what happened. Your brother does most of the talking. At first you hold back a smile: you did something bad. But as he continues talking, you realize what you probably already know, that this should not have happened. Your dad is concerned. He wants to make sure you're both okay. Sure, you're okay. And then it's done. When your dad leaves, your brother and you probably shrug it off. Then it goes away. No one says anything more about it.

But the brothers down the block catch wind of it when your brother teases casually, because both of you are uncomfortable with it. And from where you were standing, neither of you can see all the shame that's around the corner. He sees the nail, you see the toe, but it turns out to be a giant that followed you home. No one else ever sees it. You already have a habit of hiding things in your slowly filling bottle of emotions, and you bury this deep and seal it up tight.

The kid who lived across the alley from you dies of a heroine overdose a dozen or so years later. He stays at a YMCA across town where they find him. You admit a sense of relief. You will never run into to him in the library, or confront him at a party. You will never have mutual friends or common interests. You won't ever see him again, you and him, the seedling of your shame.

CHAPTER 7
Dealing with the Daemon Anger

The leaves did not catch at first. Perry's hands were always a little shaky and it wasn't until he concentrated did they still long enough for the lighter to still long enough for the flame to catch the dry leaves piled across the length of the gutter. Perry had crooked eyes too, which were hard to see past his squinty lids. The blond barn hay on his head may have housed a few small birds, and he lost his finger in the garage door when he was little, but his father put it on ice, gave him three shots of whiskey, and sped him to the hospital in time for them to sew it back on.

He stomped on the flame before it got out of hand. Wylie graveled a laugh. Leaf took the lighter and lit the pile again. He let it burn. The three faces glowed in the flame, not blue, but *orange*. Leaf saw blue when he played; but orange was real. The heat was real, the smoke was real, the disintegrating leaves were real. Perry squawked a laugh and began stomping the leaf pile. Wylie backed his bike away slowly with a grin. The flame seemed to dodge his scampering feet. Leaf joined in.

His heart raced, but in a good way, and Leaf wasn't scared, he was excited. He stomped and stomped, then threw his book bag down to smolder the flame. Gray smoke plumed from under his back pack and the three coughed relief. That was close; lately things were getting closer and closer.

They continued on toward the Woods and the classes that would start soon, Wylie on his bike, flanked by Leaf on his bike, then Perry, who was walking close behind. They talked about Mr. Stankowitz and how he made fun of Daoud for being fat, in front of the whole class. It angered Perry that he always did that.

"He's a dick," Wylie said.

Leaf told them that when his older sister Margie had him for a teacher, a girl in her class put a picture of his head on a popsicle stick and said she had *Stank-on-a-Stick*. They felt a little better, made Stankowitz feel smaller to them.

Wylie said that Leaf's back pack *stank* from the fire he put out with it. Leaf smelled it and jerked his head back. Perry wanted to smell for himself. *Yep, that stank.* It was unanimous. Leaf tried to beat the stank out, but the vinyl was charred and the stank was embedded. He said his mom was going to think he was smoking. Wylie pointed out that, for a little bit, he was smoking.

Perry asked, "You got cigarettes?" He lagged behind, not fully engaged, wandering almost automatically into it. He weaved back and forth as he walked, head flopping around, eyes still crooked. He skipped a little to catch up, and glanced back at the leaf pile.

Although a block away, he could see it clearly because it glowed with a six-foot orange flame, and the smoke rose from it as if to signal its success *(Distress!)*. He stopped and turned around to face it.

"The leaves!"

Wylie rode forward a little before turning the wheel to stop. Leaf turned and stopped. He had only seen a blue flame that big before, but he was beginning to think blue flames were bullshit. Blue never burned anything, never smoked, never stank, never really en*Danger*ed.

Danger! As if they were all tapped into that same thought, like a herd of cattle, they broke, and sprinted for cover. And they were gone. Only the quiet chewing of the leaf pile remained, until a neighbor stepped out onto his porch, let out yelp, and ran back the way he came.

Peeking out from around the brick, between two deep-red apartment buildings, the boys let the sirens scream for them, the neighbors do the gawking, and left the extinguishing to the firemen, but the story, they saved for themselves. And they swam in it all the way to the Woods, leaving no reaction unrealized, no stomach-turn unturned, and no plot-detail unthickened. Orange was better than blue. It was unanimous.

They split up when they got to school, entering the building from different doors to avoid being spotted in a pack. Leaf stuffed his stanky bag into his locker and pulled out a math book. It was eighth-grade math and he was the only seventh-grader in the class, but a few of them had known his brother from the year before, so no one held it against him. He played a quiet role in the class, respectful, attentive, humble.

Occasionally late was the only time he didn't

blend right in, really the only evidence of a boy behind the moderate facade of student. That flaw seemed to define him more than anything, as flaws often do, gave definition, gave meaning.

Mr. Darin's back was facing the chalkboard as Leaf entered the classroom. The class saw him, but the teacher did not. Leaf felt himself pulled forward out of the flat backdrop of the classroom as the eyes of eighth-grade girls recognized those definitions in his character, that lapse between what they thought they knew and what they didn't know. He knew what they didn't know, and it glared orange from behind his thick lop-sided spectacles and wide eyes.

He answered correctly the next question that was asked of him. The average speed of a train traveling 57 miles per hour northbound which slows to 32 miles per hour west through the Woods, arriving at the station 7 minutes late. A few calculations in his head, he got that from his mom, who once proved Pi to the umpteenth decimal place. Beep boop bop boop beep boop bop. These were things he thought about in his sleep.

Henry slept through the repeated calls from his mom to get up, and Leaf had closed the door behind him when he'd left, so the room was presumed empty, and Henry just slept in. His mind was gone until the last moment when his eyes opened and he was yanked back into his bedroom. *Was this his bedroom?*

"Fuck." Henry saw the clock past nine thirty. He didn't like it when he was late by accident; he lost credibility, to himself. He twisted his tired body, cracked his neck, and sat on the edge of his bed. The red mark from a crease in his pillow case divided his face in two: the red for the shame, and the pale for the effort it took to conceal it.

He carried that world around with him. It was heavier than most, and many daughters had insisted on taking it off his shoulders. They've asked and they've told and they've pleaded and they've even tried to coax Henry away from the world on his shoulders, but Henry wouldn't have it. He carried the load himself, and the daughters may have wept, but Henry would carry the load alone. So, his body always ached and his neck always cracked.

Henry pissed out an ocean, hocked up an island and threw on the clothes he'd worn the day before. He grabbed his coat from inside the closet, above the metal chest where he hid things, and made a bee-line to school, leaving behind any hint of inquiry, any engagement with the daughters, any recollection of the other side, but bringing, as always, the whole world with him, just like he brought his big shit-kicker boots. And just as he wouldn't let Leaf wear his big shit-kicker boots, he wouldn't let Leaf carry his world either, not one ounce of it. Even though it belonged to both of them, he'd be damned if he'd have Leaf carry any of it. He carried it so Leaf wouldn't have to.

He smoked a cigarette outside the gym doors by

himself and waited for the next bell to ring so he could slip into the hallways during the passing period. As the smoke crept up through his fingers, up past his eyes, he noticed a light in his periphery, as if the smoke gave it form, revealed it from hiding. His eye darted to see it, but it was gone. Maybe it wasn't a light, maybe it was a reflection of a light, but it reminded him of something, a thought, or a feeling he'd had before, an emotion that swept over him and washed through his entire field of vision. This light, this reflection was the residual of a girl, a daughter, *the* daughter.

Maybe he did remember one engagement with the daughter, maybe it was the dance, maybe it was her breasts, but her breasts during the dance, and maybe that's what he was drawing instead of taking notes during Consumer Ed. Not just the curve of her breasts though, the curve of her whole body, the movement of her whole body. His pencil etched out the movement of her whole body on white paper. And for a moment, he was back in the courtyard, dancing with the daughter and the daughter's breasts. He did this without dozing off; he did this while he was wide awake, and it was nice to see her again. It was nice to once again dance with the Queen Lizard's daughter. It was nice to once again know who she was.

Henry floated to his next class. He had forgotten his wings, who knew where, but he floated to his next class. He floated by Clem shooting craps with a small group students in a back hallway. Clem stood up off of one knee and watched Henry as Henry watched him back. He smiled and waved, deciding then to pop outside for a smoke, to take the opportunity and remember. He remembered flying over the stadium, and he remembered climbing to the roof of the Glow Home, and he remembered Dr. Soloman, with the long beard that he couldn't cut, but just kept growing and growing. But then it was gone, it had returned to his periphery, and he could only remember remembering.

After school, Henry met his friends on the Hill, and Jen was there and Giggles was there and so was Ken, who was a little man, but there weren't many men in high school, little or not. Henry didn't want to tell them about the Queen Lizard's daughter, especially not Ken. Ken was busy telling about how he was once possessed by an old man who picked apples for a living but died in his sleep from a skin disease, and Ken spent the entire night on the roof scratching every little itch he could find. He woke up in the morning with scabs all over his legs and a shingle tile print on his cheek that didn't go away for a three days.

Especially not Ken. He didn't want to cheapen it by turning it into an anecdote, so he told them about how he saw Clem shooting craps with a small group of students in a back hallway, and how Clem broke 'em up when he saw Henry, and he tried to cover it up, but Henry knew, and Clem knew he knew. So, he gave Clem a big smile and lit up his cigarette a good ten yards before the door.

"What a suck-ass," Giggles said of Clem

"Cops, man. They're just criminals with

a badge." Ken said this, then spit to the ground the phlegm that he'd been rolling around on his tongue. He regaled them with his story of being pulled over with an ounce of weed in his glove box and the illegal search that fruitlessly followed, ignoring Giggles when he made the distinction between a cop and a high school security guard.

Giggles added, "I don't know if he's a criminal; he's definitely a suck-ass," and then giggled.

"All I know is next time he gives us shit about smoking, I'm gonna flick that cigarette at him, tell him I'll tell my mom all about the gambling ring he runs in the school," Henry warned. Ken said he should tell the Superintendent, working Henry into a frenzy. "Yeah, I'd tell the Superintendent, man. Get his ass fired!" Ken said he should "get that fucker fired!" There was fire in his tone, and it was infectious, catching hold of the boys who considered pain to be the threshold to manhood. Not that they all believed it, but they definitely considered it. All except Jen, who was boyish, but would never cross that threshold, and never intended to.

"Flick the cigarette at his face?" she began to Henry with a sassy side smile, "Prolly not..."

It was a smile that always brought him down a notch. If Giggles had said it, he'd have gone up two notches, but Jen could steer a tone, that was her gift. When there was silence her mind raced, and she was uncomfortable, but when there was chaos, she didn't have to move and could think clearly, and stand firm, calm. She had an inflection and a confidence that cleared the way for a humble response. She knew what they all knew somewhere, Truth was the threshold, and it was both painful and beautiful. There was a pause, from everyone. Henry obliged.

"Well, probably not... I'd probably just mutter something under my breath and put out my cigarette." That got a chuckle. He smiled, pretended to bring it up a notch, and pointed at Jen, who took a drag of her cigarette. "But, God-dammit, when he'd walked away, I'd pick that cigarette up off the ground and smoke the shit out of it." That got some laughs.

"As you should, Henry, it's *your* cigarette," Jen approved from behind the laughs.

"And then eat the butt just to spite him," Giggles said, then laughed. Henry turned a light shade of red, grinned from ear to ear and laughed like a harlequin. Even Ken was grinning a bit. Somewhere, he appreciated the opportunity to bring himself down a notch.

Jen and Henry slipped away when Ken tackled Giggles in an uproar of gawking laughter, having teased him one too many times for paying a hundred twenty bucks for his big black boots. It was "you fuckin' yuppie," then Ken's forearm pressing on Giggle's head until it hurt, and Giggles throwing him off. He was a full two sizes bigger than Ken, but he didn't like to throw his weight around. He found out early on that a combination of his mind and mouth were more effective, and required much less effort, and the giggling just came naturally. But sometimes Ken went too far.

Jen pulled out two smokes. She gave one to

Henry.

"Thanks." He lit his with a quick snap of his Zippo, *clink*, and left it lit for hers. They stopped walking for the steady, then continued a moment after her cigarette had ignited. He snapped the lighter closed, *clink*. They each took a drag and let it circulate in the lungs.

When they were far enough away from the park, Jen started telling Henry about the weird dreams she's been having lately. She might never actually fall asleep, but she did dream.

"Yeah, like what?"

"I don't really remember, but some of them were with you in 'em, but we were little kids."

Henry laughed and looked at her. "What were we doing?"

"I don't know, there was like this room that was a library and I was trying to tell a story, but I don't remember what the story was or why I was telling it, but it was so important that everyone listened. I was so close to... to getting control."

"Well, what was I doing?"

"You were this kid like running around, making all this noise. And you had this little bow and arrow, but they were paper arrows. And there were like four or five of you. And I think I got fed up and I threw one of you down onto these rocks."

"You threw me? Why'd you throw me?"

"I don't know, you were this little fucking kid, that was making all this noise. And I was trying to tell you a story."

"I would *not* let you baby-sit for me."

"Stop, I'm not kidding. I was so angry, and I just picked you up and threw you. I felt really bad afterwards."

"Oh, well, then it's okay." (Sarcasm.)

Jen smiled, "Come on, Henry. You deserve to be picked up and thrown sometimes." Henry took another drag of his cigarette and let it circulate the lungs.

"Yeah, I guess that's true." In his head, Henry picked himself up as a child. His child self kicked and screamed and stubbornly tried to wriggle away. His shoes clopped his forehead and scuffed his cheek. His little outstretched hands grabbed a clump of his hair, screaming and crying and trying his best to fight. Henry felt the pain beneath his scalp, at his roots, and he filled with rage toward that stubborn fuckin' kid, that fucking' little devil. He hurled his child self off a cliff to the rocks below. The impact was enough to pull him right back to the street with Jen.

"Let's go to the Mill," he said. Jen said nothing, only followed when Henry turned to head west of the park. She'd seen him go somewhere in his head, and she knew he went somewhere she couldn't.

After he ordered his coffee, he sat across from the globular sculpture next to the cream, sugar, and lids. Jen got hers too. She sat across from him, both facing out from the wall, not toward each other, but toward the burned out core of the Mill.

"Sorry I threw you off the cliff," Jen said as

off-handed as she could. Henry broke his repose for a moment and smiled at her. But after the moment, he turned back to his thoughts and the thing that had pulled him gravitationally. He felt an electrical pulse course over his skin. His shoulders and his neck sagged under the weight.

"That's alright," he said, "I probably would've done the same."

Jen took a sip of her coffee. She mentally ingested the melted-down hunk of metal by the cream, sugar, and lids. She wondered how hot it had to be to melt a thing like that. *Pretty fucking hot*, she decided. Hot like *hell-hot*.

"What the *hell* did you think you were doing?!" Mr. Alfonse raised his voice, but he didn't have to. His voice was always one of reprimand, no matter at what volume. Small for his age, Leaf looked all the more small in the singular chair opposite the vice-principal's desk. He was called in for fire, but not for the morning leaf fire. The thing about orange flames was that they kept calling, and one fed the other. His eyes shifted behind his thick lop-sided spectacles. The door to the office was closed. He shrugged his little shoulders.

"I don't know."

"I don't know? Well, that's obvious. It was stupid. Stupid! Lighting fireworks in the back of the bus. Are you nuts, kid? Are you frickin' nuts?" Leaf thought this question might be rhetorical, but Mr. Alfonse waited for an answer, the moment measured by a pulsing vein bulging from his neck.

"No."

"Then you're just stupid. I can not believe the gall of you kids. You better be glad Ms. Jenkins turned that bus around and called me, instead of calling the cops, because your ass would be in Juvie right now. Juvie! You hear me?"

What he heard was *gall*. Leaf said nothing. He just stared at the front of the desk from behind his thick lopsided spectacles, and peeked up every so often at Mr. Alfonse's burning red face to show that he was sufficiently shamed. He caught the intense eyes, clenched in their sockets, never blinking, and quickly looked away.

"That's not even your bus. What the hell were you doing on that bus? How did you get on?"

"I don't know, I just walked on." Although it was Perry who handed him his bus pass out the window. And Perry had lit the fireworks, but only because Leaf couldn't get the lighter to work, neither had really meant to. Mr. Alfonse was right about one thing: they hadn't given it much thought. It was just the fire that drew them near, and then they got excited.

"Detention, all this week and next, after school, 'til four thirty."

Leaf gave no protest. "Okay."

"And I'm going to have a long talk with your parents." He could have mentioned that he knew them well from the times that Henry got caught smoking in the bathroom and ditching class, but he didn't. His blood was boiling from this boy, and he wanted to stay in that moment. It was, after all, his role as administrator that made him feel important, made him feel useful.

As he exited the office, Leaf caught the eye of Wylie, sitting in the waiting chairs. Perry sat next to him, his hand covering his mouth. Leaf tried not to smile, but Wylie always got a smirk on his face when he was uncomfortable, and the trying made it that much more irrepressible. Leaf squeezed his eyes shut as the huge grin grew across his face, but Wylie was the one facing Mr. Alfonse and even though his eyes went to the ground, the corner of his tightly-pressed mouth curled up from the pressure, holding his breath to suppress a laugh.

"Mr. Soskin! Wipe that grin off your face! Perry, get in here!" yelled Mr. Alfonse.

Perry got whiny, "What?! I wasn't doing anything."

"Get in here! Close the door!" Perry did, but sneaked a smirk back out at Leaf as he closed the door. Leaf left the office and Wylie, who was under the watchful eye of Old Ms. Jeffrey, the vice-principal's secretary. As he swaggered down the hall he heard the gravely laugh of Wylie Soskin erupt. Old Ms. Jeffrey asked if she was going to have to interrupt the meeting with a one-word warning. "Wylie?!"

Mr. Alfonse let them out fifteen minutes apart so they couldn't walk home together. He held Wylie Soskin the longest because he was the cockiest, saving his best for last, yelling until he could turn no more red, until all his veins bulged and streaked his throat like the exposed roots of a tree, and on the way home he had Wylie fighting back the tears he would never have shown in the office. He saved his best for last, and yet may never have known the marks his tongue thrashing left. Under the heat, he'd forgotten that he was a grown man and that Wylie was a boy. It was easy to forget in the Woods.

Leaf, who had never been any trouble before, walked out of the Woods first. He was a train headed southbound at 57 miles per hour, steam building, a line of smoke trailing behind. It rained a little, maybe a residual effect from the fall of the Committee, maybe not, but Leaf felt a sense of hope anyway. Not one that made him smile, one that made it easier to scowl,

One that made it easier to keep that scowl through the night and into the morning so that he didn't even notice when Forehead passed by him at lunch, watching him closely for a sign of entry, a reason to headlock. Leaf was thinking about those things that made him scowl and those things to which he was entitled and those things that Mr. Alfonse was trying to take from him, and Forehead never found an entry and just continued on.

But Leaf did notice after Forehead passed. He noticed that he'd ignored him. He was thinking to himself, and he'd ignored him. Leaf almost felt a little bad, almost got up and offered him his head for a headlock, but he stayed put. He remembered what

Nobody had told AJua about him being scared. Scared of what, he thought. He watched Forehead as he waywardly wandered the perimeter of the playground, running his hand along the fence, holding a conversation with himself, just like Leaf.

I wasn't scared, Leaf thought, *I was just his headlockee, so that he could be a headlocker, instead of a wayward wanderer.*

But I was scared. Of being a wayward wanderer too. Anything to not wander aimlessly.

I thought I was just being nice.

I wasn't being nice; I was being selfish.

I thought I was lost.

But I'm not lost, I'm not wayward. I know where I want to be! The orange fire lights the way!

Why are you wayward, Forehead, when the Orange fire lights the dark corners of these Woods?

It's draws out and defines. I been to the fucking Rope Fields. I climbed to the top of the Topless Trees. I saw the Heart of the Mill.

No, I was in the heart of the mill, I were the gears to the heart of the mill. It was not Henry, but me who was lain face down in the flames of its heart as it ran, turned, cranked and burned me with Black Electricity.

I will not be wayward.

I will not be selfish.

I'm gonna burn it, he thought, *I'm gonna burn the Woods down.*

Leaf brought his hand to his own forehead, which chimed with a red glow. He brought his hand down past the tiny apple in his throat, and stopped at his heart, the heart that beat so fast sometimes. Then across the breadth of his shoulders, bone to bone, from where he spoke to AJua. But AJua had already heard him. And not even Nobody cried.

He lit it from underneath, to get it going.

He lit an uncurled paper clip until it glowed red. He burned a smiley face into his arm. He pressed it against his right forearm, and a head formed and two eyes and a smile, branded forever with a smile. He would no longer be sad. And then Wylie, and William & the Hatch Boys, and Bjorn burned one as well, some not sure why, some knowing exactly why, some used ice, some let it smoke.

"You smell like smoke."

Leaf had arrived twenty minutes late for a dinner at the giant oak oval table. Leaf sat across from Anne Marie, and he and Anne Marie and his mom and his pop made four. Henry was not yet home. It was his mom who smelled the smoke. It was his mom with the keenest sense of smell.

"I know, Bjorn's mom smokes," Leaf confessed.

The chicken casserole was a little cold, but the peas and carrots and mashed potatoes still melted butter. His mom began to prepare him a plate. His pop, with a mouthful of mashed potatoes and wheat bread, asked what Bjorn's last name was. Bread and potatoes.

"Lindson. Where's Henry?" Leaf reached half-way for the orange juice. Anne Marie handed it the rest of the way.

"Winston?" Still bread and potatoes.

"Lind-son." Enunciating as he poured.

"Henry's eating at Joseph's and your sister's at rehearsal," his mom said and scooped the casserole.

"Oh, that's right. Lindson. And his mother's name?" Last of the bread and potatoes.

"Linda." Leaf said at the end of a long sip.

"Linda Lindson. Oh, brother…" His pop laughed as bread and potatoes pocketed in his cheeks.

"Beets?" his mother asked.

"No," urgent and "thank you," trying not to sound so urgent.

"I'll give you one."

"Pop, can I have a sip of your beer?" Anne Marie wanted to know.

"Alright, just a little one. And what's his father's name?"

"Thank you." Leaf received the plate from his mom with open palms. Anne Marie received the beer from the large stein with wide eyes. Her sip was small, but her face still bittered with a smile, and she set the stein back to its original setting. "I don't know. He doesn't live with his dad. Can I have a sip of your beer, too?"

His pop waved his hand in annoyance, "Go ahead."

Leaf grabbed the stein and began a sip, like the orange juice sip, lasting longer than it should.

"Leaf!" His mom quipped.

His father barked, "A sip! I said a sip."

Leaf pulled the stein from his mouth with a smile, causing Anne Marie to put her hand over her own. He set the stein back to its original setting.

"Now, why do you do that? I said a sip." Cheeks no longer full of bread and potato.

"Hmm, it's pretty good."

"Yeah, well, I better not catch you drinking any more of that," warned his mom.

"I won't." She served him his plate and things settled. "Shall we pray?" Everyone crossed themselves. Tonight, he wished Henry were here with them. Then out came the one word prayer:

B l e s s u s O L o r d f o r t h e s e t h y g i f t s w h i c h w e a r e a b o u t t o r e c e i v e t h r o u g h y o u r b o u n t y t h r o u g h C h r i s t o u r L o r d A m e n 'N a m e o f t h e F a t h e r t h e S o n a n d H o l y S p i r i t...

Leaf touched his forehead, cut his face in two as he drew his hand down to his heart, what he was and what he'd hoped to become, then lopped his head off across his shoulders, for all the chaos it would bring. *Amen*!

The room paused until they all finished, then picked up right where it left off, more conversation, more questions.

What was it about the curve in Jen's back as she reached back to turn on the record player? She was sitting on the edge of her bed, and the side of her shirt pulled up with her arm, and Henry had seen that crescented curve before. It took him by surprise the way it grabbed him and held him, familiar and yet unfamiliar, because Jen was familiar and the curve was familiar, but before that moment, the two had not been familiar together. He felt a little dizzy and a little distant when she turned back to him.

"I just got this from Val's."

"Val's Halla?" That was all he could think to say, but he knew it was. What other Val's? Jen always picked up the sweet vinyl from Val's Halla Record Shop.

She didn't answer, she was listening to the scratchy drum beat and distorted guitars. In the air, she drummed along the fill at the end of the intro, leaned back and lit a cigarette. She turned to look at him and he'd gone somewhere else, which she was used to, but he was looking at her as he went. She smiled and drummed out another fill. He smiled too, lit his own cigarette. *Clink.*

He wasn't at Joseph's having dinner. He hadn't been to Joseph's house in years, but he was a friend from the old neighborhood, and his Mom knew him. He'd kept a little bit of truth from her, because he was getting better at it. He'd kept a little for himself, and it helped him to feel more defined, gave him the courage to stay with, not just the curves, but the relief that they promised.

"You brought this back with you, from Val's," Henry spoke on empty. Val was a big ex-hippie with an enormous natural perm, lots of cats, and a hallway of a music store that took in and welcomed most of the wayward teens at one time or another. Jen nodded her head to the beat. Henry had worked for her for a brief period until the two got a chance to talk and realized they had nothing in common, further, they didn't even like each other, further, it became apparent that big ex-hippies with enormous natural perms and lots of cats were easily irritated by fifteen year-olds who might already know everything there is to know. He didn't go in there anymore. He always felt guilty, like all of it was his fault, and he just added it to the world he carried on his shoulders. "Can I see the cover?"

She stretched back once more to slide the cover off the shelf. This time Henry got pins and needles on his shoulders, as he matched her curve to fit perfectly with the one etched in his mind. She saw him this time. She put out her cigarette and, with the album cover, leaned back next to him against the wall, so they both could read it. He could smell her hair. He could feel his long-lashed lids lose themselves in outer space where there is no gravity. Henry'd kissed girls before, even touched a small breast or two, but he didn't ever fly to their rooftops and watch them dance and listen to them sing. He didn't listen to their stories. He never got pins and needles across his shoulders, where he carried this world, morning, noon and night, this world which made him grow so old, so young.

Jen pulled the strands of her jet black hair behind her ear, so she could listen to the rhythm in his breath. He was looking past the album cover, and he was elsewhere.

"I can't get anything from there," he said. "From Val's."

"Tell me what you want. I'll get it for you. I'll bring it back with me." Her response was without hesitation and it touched Henry to the point where he wanted to tell her what he wanted, but he couldn't speak. He'd lost his voice. But if she would bridge the gap, if she would bring back what he couldn't. *Wait*, what if she couldn't, what makes him think that she's even able? He looked at her and she read that fear in his eyes behind his long-lashed lids that floated in outer space.

"Val can be a bitch sometimes," Jen said, which meant that it wasn't all his fault, and a small piece of that world ate itself. It was just a small piece, but to a world where nothing ever disappeared but just kept adding and adding, Henry felt the difference. And the fear left, and then it was only his eyes looking at hers, and then she kissed him with her mouth open.

The world of guilt and shame that Henry carried on his shoulders did not disappear, but he did set it on the shelf next to the record player while he made out with Jen. With every kiss he felt a little more relief, with every touch of her curves he felt a little less afraid and a little closer to a place where he once freely flew to and from. And he didn't have a cigarette on his way home in the dark, but rather marveled at the strength of his shoulders and neck, and how much easier it was to bear his burden after the hour and a half of not. He marveled at how she'd made a piece of his world eat itself. And the inside of his head continued to play that sweet vinyl that she'd brought back from Val's Halla.

CHAPTER 8
the Sacrificial Boy

Over the next few months, while Henry was making out with Jen, Leaf was burning down the woods little by little. Each wanted to tell the other of the new excitement they'd found, the days without day for Henry, and the illuminated darkness for Leaf, but their excitement had a hold of its own, and each was consumed by it.

Leaf didn't even see AJua much during that time. He followed the Orange fire, and joined others led by the same. He had developed an inquisitive nature, a thirst for details. The details that he found most intriguing burned inside the laughter and gazes of girls and the little breasts that they grew. And the friendship that he learned from Wylie and Perry grew, encompassing *William & the Hatchboys* and Bjorn, the tall blonde Swede, and the girls from south of the Running River.

AJua waited patiently, watching, smiling, sitting at the foot of Leaf's bed, even if Leaf didn't see him. He cried, but mostly because he was happy to see Leaf engaged. He was happy to see Leaf excited to wake in the morning, as he was excited to go to sleep at night, too thirsty to be afraid.

But as Leaf put his fear aside, it didn't mean that it went away. It just didn't get as much play time, with all the other moments queued on the playlist. The moments played in succession, without interruption, without repetition. Leaf first danced with the eighth-grader in the headband from his math class. She asked him to dance, and when the MC said swing your partner round and round, he did just that. And when the MC said do-si-do, Leaf did-si-did. And every three weeks or so it was time to change partners, and Leaf reluctantly changed, but after the third or fourth time, he was getting the hang of it.

Wylie got a handjob from Wendy. Leaf touched the top part of Lindsay's breast while they made out on the couch. Even Perry french-kissed a Paula, who had perfectly-straight eyes. Most of *William & the Hatchboys* danced, a few watched, but most danced. Bjorn danced a tall blonde Swedish dance, and everyone switched partners with the girls from the south. There was always music playing and there was always someone to dance with. Everyone was so excited to dance. Leaf understood, to dance was to live, and to live in the moment.

But in order to stay in the moment, which seemed to accelerate at an inordinate pace, Leaf had to skip, and then trot, and then run.

Wylie Soskin got the Canadian Whiskey from his eldest brother. He met Leaf at the house where he was dog-sitting for a couple who knew his parents. They had a son, but he was off in the military. They also had vodka in their freezer and a whole cellar full of wine. William, of *William & the Hatchboys*, met them soon after. He brought his Cheshire smile, a smile so big that when he flashed it all of the trouble around him disappeared. Leaf once saw him take a punch in the side of the head that reared a knot only moments later. Leaf liked him right away.

The punch came from Leon, an eighth grader who had a girlfriend that William put his arm around once, but William put his arm around everyone, and his intentions were *a picture of garage light glistening off the dew of the red bud blossoms.* But Leon covered those with the dark of his own intentions. Backed by eight of his friends, egging, taunting, goading for a fight, Leon puffed up his feathers and danced like a *Jet* from *West Side Story.* This was despite William's best efforts to ease him down a notch with his humble, dignified apology.

Leon was scared, scared of doing the wrong thing in front of the crowd, William was not. It seemed the wrong thing to Leon was backing down, because he snapped and *Pop!* right in the side of the head. Hands in his pocket, William took the punch, then righted his head. He waited for a moment while Leon tried to hide the glint of shame that shone in his eye. Leaf and Perry stood behind him, outnumbered, out-muscled and without enough bile inside of them. Rob joined them, but not to fight, just to distance himself from the crowd.

William turned and walked away; the three followed. It didn't take more than twenty feet before the Cheshire smile grew on his face, allowing the others to do the same, leaving the crowd of congratulatory gawkers to dust. *Did it leave a mark?*, he asked his friends. *There's already a knot*, said Leaf. William's hand unstuck from his pocket to touch the tender side of his forehead. *You took it like a man*, said Rob, who once fit a quarter in his nose. *What am I gonna tell my mom?*, William thought out loud as he smiled through the pain, as if he'd bumped his head. *You could tell her you ran into a pole*, said Perry. Leaf was already telling the story in his head, the day William got popped on the side of the forehead, and simply walked away.

William walked up the front walk and met Wylie and Leaf at the dog sitting house as they'd planned a week before. Leaf had already poured himself a rootbeer and vodka with no ice, of which he took wincing sips at the kitchen table as Wylie prepared two glasses of cranberry and vodka for himself and William.

This tastes awful, Leaf had warned them of the rootbeer mixture. The three talked excitedly in anticipation of the buzz they knew was coming, but had never actually experienced. They talked of how it tasted, how it smelled, how the light of the head was coming on, how the bottles of wine lined the basement walls in rows and rows, how they'd found BBs in a drawer in the son's bedroom upstairs, but no gun. William went to explore the rest of the house, followed by the Scottish terriers (one black, one white) whose giddy excitement mirrored that of the boys.

Wylie pulled the *Canadian Club* bottle from his bag as if to present it as the main event. Leaf's eye's got wide, and he grabbed at the bottle until Wylie finally gave in. But before he could properly introduce it, Leaf unscrewed the cap and took several gulps straight from the bottle. *That's whiskey, Leaf!* And Leaf knew it as soon as it hit his belly: the Fire! His eyes burned red and swelled with water as he coughed and handed the bottle back to a laughing Wylie. *I thought it was wine from downstairs*, said Leaf. *No, it's whiskey, it's the hard shit.* Wylie took a small swig himself and breathed the fire too. William came back to the bleary-eyed pair with news of a smut film. He laughed at the story of what he'd just missed, then took a swig of the whiskey himself, passing through the fire to meet the boys on the other side. Cheshire Smile, then all the world around them disappeared.

Wylie lying on his belly half off the corner of the king size bed, unable to voice his discontentment with Leaf and William, who jumped on and off the bed all around him, dodging the BBs that the other threw, an unwatched old smut film played on the TV, equal and opposite Scottish Terriers hopping and yapping in perfect metronomic unison. Manboys exploring the depths of the woods, bellies full of fire, without fear, with community, for the sake of feeling useful. That's how it started. When it ended they were all just running around, making all this noise, shooting their paper arrows.

Leaf kept up though, and he never wished for his invisible glasses. For that, he was proud. He did, however, wish for the wings that he and Henry used to carry with them. He still got afraid when he had to stand still for too long or when he had to ask a girl out and try to kiss her. It would have been easier with the wings, to face all these new risks, but AJua was the keeper of the wings, and Leaf almost forgot who AJua was.

He remembered quickly, however, when later that summer the music stopped, and they go the news that one of the Hatchboys had been hurled off the cliff to the rocks below. Just as Henry had seen it, just as Jen dreamed it for him as she desperately tried to tell all of the little boys a story.

It was the boy William who fell, and the impact broke his neck and crushed his skull. It was the boy William who often danced with himself while most danced with partners. Those who didn't have partners, didn't dance, except William. He wasn't afraid; he knew who he was. In the same moment when Leaf wished for his wings, he wished he could dance with himself, like William did, at his own pace, to his own satisfaction. William looked like all the other Leafs, and like all the other little Henrys, but he was marked, in both worlds, for the sacrifice.

Leaf wished that he himself was marked for the sacrifice, but no one would allow that to happen to him. So, he had to separate himself. Now imagine you separating yourself, pulling this part from that part. It's safer that way, but it does get so lonely sometimes.

CHAPTER 9
the Separate Self

I rode my bike through the dark to Christine's house. I'd moved back in with my parents in the suburbs when it turned out I wasn't as close to everyone as I thought I was, and I was broke again. I worked part time at an ice cream parlor, exchanging juvenile jive with my teen-aged co-workers. My brother got a job at a bar near our Wicker Park apartment. He moved into his own place.

I gave up drinking because *the Sacrificial Victim of the Earthy People in the Entrance Hall* and myself had become one in the same, and I was now in the process of filleting that parasite from my bones. For the past two years, I had eaten little to no meat, an eating disorder I'd picked up from an ex-girlfriend, called being a *vegetarian*. My caloric intake had been cut in half. It had become the rule, not the exception, to eat when the dizziness from hunger kicked in. I starved my mind of its higher faculties and left it to primitively ache for sustenance.

My metabolism had been fueled only by alcohol and starch, and my endurance was down to that of a gaunt dog rummaging desperately through the trash for his next meal, always desperate, always for immediate satiation. Now I was left to deal with the chemical rut I had worked myself into, climbing uphill with mental muscles that had atrophied, longing for the habitual ingestion that I'd gotten used to.

Christine was my steady, the extent of which she knew little about, but my mind grinded over everything that threatened that steady. Gritting teeth, mashed nerves, and accusations, another thing she knew little about. Of her and anyone else: the guys she worked with, my best friend, my brother, even her dog, even her ten year-old cousin, even the elderly man who lived below her, even her best friend, even her and herself... *Jesus Christ, put a bullet in my fucking head!* But I was panicking and backed into a corner, protecting myself. But for what?

To protect a dream that I could no longer have, I suppose. Because to a starving man the wall between the waking world and the dreaming world thins away, and the one chews away at the other. When the body has nothing to eat, it starts to eat itself.

I rode on an old dirtbike I'd picked up for a song on ebay, a very sad song. I was much too big for the bike. But I still had that at least, my sad song. Here I am, as I was thirteen years ago, riding a dirt bike through the side streets of my home town, peered by ice-cream vending adolescents, trying desperately to hop out of the rut I had created through a pacification process that offered me no hope, no faith, nothing to build upon. Except now, I rode alone, outgrown by the rest of the world.

Back then, at least, we rode in packs. We pulled onto Jill's lawn and she came out with tears in her eyes, normally trying so hard to look older, now looking less than the twelve years she had. She said it like it wasn't fair, "Bill's dead!" We dropped our bikes.

The girls were already there, collected in Jill's kitchen as she called William's house to confirm what none of us believed. "Is Bill there?" She contested the response, but it was confirmed, and she began to cry. Bjorn had his arm around me, but then pushed me away in cries of anger. I leaned back against the counter and followed the pattern in the linoleum floor tile. Halfway in the doorway, Jenna chewed her nails furiously. It wasn't fair.

That was in June, three days before my birthday. The boy William had been dead as long as he'd been alive, I thought, and I'd forgotten to remember. The anniversary of his death was a week before. I always remembered, always observed that day. It was engraved in my bones, but I must have cut that part out while I gutted for my own *Sacrificial Victim*. My body began to shake.

I pulled my bike on my shoulder and lugged it up the three flights of stairs to set it beside the back door of Christine's condo. Outside the door, I composed myself. I let myself in, greeted by the high pitched barks of the little Shitzu-Poodle mix. Christine followed close behind, "Hi-ii". I gave her a hug, and the shakes that I tried to hold in began to come out. She pulled me closer, and the shaking was a kettle boiling, and I began to cry. I was scaring her. I sat down on a dining room chair and she held my head, "what, what is it, what's wrong?"

I shrugged, I couldn't explain it, "I forgot the

anniversary of Bill's death last week." She pulled me in closer and sighed sympathetically. But that's not what I meant. "I'm frozen," I told her. "What do you mean, you're frozen?" My head returned to her belly, then she pulled it away and made me look at her. I looked away.

"I'm stuck, I'm still a stubborn little punk. I look forward to the day when Bill died so I can use him as an excuse." She had recently lost a friend too, to colon cancer, she watched him die. "It's okay to feel sad about that, that's a painful thing." I was no longer crying, more angry and ashamed, "that was thirteen years ago. I knew him for nine months." The Shit-Poo barked because of the attention he was not getting. "Murray, No! No barking!"

I stood and got myself a glass of water. We sat on the couch and watched TV the rest of the night, Christine and Murray and I, and she put up the gate when we went to bed and calmly said, "No, Murray, we can't all go," and although I knew she was talking to the dog, I took from it what I needed to hear.

We slept squished together on her twin bed, her hand on the light patch of hair on my chest, but I felt like a little boy. I hid my eyes from the street light that shone in through the bamboo blinds. I normally talked to the boy William when I was up at night and thinking about him, but I couldn't talk to him now. He was part of me now, and I knew it.

"Buck up," he would say when I was down, just like when he was alive. I held him above the rest, separated him. He'd helped usher me through the woods, an even child in a world beyond my understanding. Even after he dies, he was still there with me.

He must have been a part of something greater, I thought, and I held that time in my life as something to which to aspire, the time when I was closest to them, all of them. But that left me aspiring to be a manboy, aspiring to repeat the same story, to relive the same pain, to continually experience truth without understanding. In death, he was trying to tell me, and I wouldn't listen, because I refused to bring that part of me close enough to verify(!).

CHAPTER 10
I WILL GIVE YOU WHAT YOU'VE LOST!

Leaf arrived twenty minutes late for a dinner at the giant oak oval table. Henry was there and so was Anne Marie, his mom, and his pop. His older sister Margie had even skipped rehearsal to be home when her brother arrived. His supper was cold. He missed grace, and was under no watchful eye to make it up. The eyes that watched him were in anticipation of the carefully hidden lament of a boy who prematurely lost a friend.

Nonetheless, Leaf crossed himself and thought about where he might send a prayer and to whom and what good it might do. He could only picture William's face in the coffin with make-up on and no expression at all. His hands were crushed or mushed or manipulated to fold on his chest, and they held a guitar pick that his older brother had put there. But it wasn't William any more, and Leaf knew it.

Henry looked at his brother from across the table, thinking of all the weight that Leaf now carried that he could not hold for him. He had imagined *himself* as the sacrificial boy; Jen had dreamed it. That's how he saw it. But it wasn't so. He was passed by for another boy, a William, an innocent. Henry did not understand.

There was a shock to the death that had to run its course before anything else. Margie asked questions, drew him out, she was good at that. She asked about it in a way that Leaf did not feel self-conscious telling.

Leaf engaged himself in his story as he told of the details he had learned, and the events surrounding, and the events that followed, mostly involving William's family, but also himself and his friends. Anne Marie had no smile to put her hand over, her eyes read of fear more than anything.

Leaf ate his dinner, and didn't excuse himself early, although he did excuse himself eventually. He took with him his slowly filling bottle of emotions and retreated up the back stairs with it. When he got inside his room, he closed the door, and when he got inside the closet, he closed that door too. He sat in the dark on the metal chest where Henry hid things, and he handed the bottle to AJua. But AJua handed it back.

He said, "Nobody thinks it should be opened by you."

Leaf shook his head, and held his breath for fear if he breathed the bottle would open. AJua looked down at him with loving fear. Leaf's eyes peeked up through the dark, sank into AJua's, and pulled Nobody out into the closet with them. The three of them sat, face to face, each with a hand on the bottle. The three made a circle with the bottle in the center.

"We'll open it together," Nobody whispered. Leaf felt so warm, and in love. Their hands became one. They turned the cap slowly, but the emotions inside, under heavy pressure, sparked and erupted like a bolt of lightning, and all Leaf could manage through the gasps of breath, as the tears ran from his eyes, dammed no more, was *Thank you. Thank you, AJua. Thank you,*

Nobody. Thank you, William. Thank you for the tears that heave so hard that it brings pain to my stomach. Thank you for the pain, thank you for the truth.

Leaf stood in the darkness of the closet and turned back to the metal chest on which he'd sat, the metal chest where Henry hid things. Leaf knew now that he too hid things in the metal chest. He placed his hands on either side of the chest. Slowly, he opened the lid and looked inside.

He saw what Henry had seen when he looked past the door, beyond the panel into the Heart of the Mill. He saw where he had been keeping the *black electricity*, where he'd tried to hide it. Like his brother, Leaf heard soft sighs of mistrust, the drone of a world uncovered, the spinning motor of a dream displaced. And the truth ran through him like the ripple of a rock in a puddle, but like the ripple of a rock that turned the puddle to stone, and Leaf almost turned to stone. But he was stronger now, and AJua and Nobody wouldn't let him. He remembered.

He remembered the truth of it. He remembered Exam Day, and he remembered that both he and Henry had failed. He saw Nobody sodomized, and he saw Henry look away, but Henry was more of a boy than Leaf had ever seen him. They were both just boys. And where was Leaf, how did he feel? He felt like Nobody. He felt like the little boy who was taken in by Doctor Soloman to learn the truth.

But when he saw the Doctor, he saw that he was no Doctor at all. He was just a boy too, like the others, but aged by the workings of his mind, the labor of his nerves, the toil of his obsession and cultivation of Black Electricity.

All that work to create power, when all he had to do was ask. The Queen Lizard's daughter would have surely shared, but in Luciferian defiance he went it alone.

Leaf looked further into the chest and saw a different part of the story. For the first time the words were not locked in place, and there was an amendment. He saw what happened to his brother Henry, while he himself was exiled to the Rope Fields. He saw it in the drawings of the curves Henry's pencil had etched out of bone-white paper, revealing movement. He told it to himself as he sat beside himself.

Henry squeezed through the red dingy bars, which had not been in the neighbor's yard an hour before, which he'd not seen the Most Wonderful Woman pull apart to make room for a small boy, of which Leaf had tried to warn him but didn't have the voice. He squeezed through the bars because he smelled the warmth on the other side, the warmth whose collision with the cool night air caused a negative draft, a pulling. Also, because he knew what that warmth meant.

He'd just witnessed the soft sighs of mistrust, the drone of a world uncovered, the spinning motor of a dream displaced on the day without day, Exam Day.

But this Exam Day did not last one day. This Exam Day lasted seven years, and he listened to the spinning motor of a dream displaced for seven years. He captured in his ear the seven-year transference of the Heart of the Mill. He was seven-year exposed to Black Electricity.

Leaf tried to whisper a warning into Henry's deaf ear, "Come back, Henry. Come back," but it was too late. And how does one whisper for seven years? What does a seven-year whisper sound like? Leaf whispered for one year, but he became exhausted, and he became disenchanted, and he saved his breath for breathing, because the part of him that normally breathed by itself was busy taking care of other parts of him. *So, breathe!* He had to remember to breathe.

He had no voice to warm Henry about the Most Wonderful Woman, no voice to tell him after seven years of not. That was Leaf's failing, but also Henry's first sacrifice. If the Most Wonderful Woman caught hold of Henry and made him tell the truth, she could not catch hold of Leaf and make him tell the truth. Henry knew that Leaf was not ready to tell the truth, that the truth was much too painful for a boy such as Leaf to tell. The truth without understanding would have killed him.

Instead, Henry resisted telling the truth as the most wonderful woman caught hold of him and hugged him and rocked him gently back and forth in her most wonderful rocking chair as he stubbornly kicked and bit and scratched and furiously struggled to be let go. The most wonderful woman had a hug that was much too strong, and she held tight through the kicks and bites and scratches until Henry had furiously struggled himself to exhaustion. Back and forth, back and forth. And Henry was still.

Back and forth, back and forth. And Henry was dizzy. Back and forth and back and forth. And Henry poured the truth from his eyes, poured the truth all over the most wonderful woman's most wonderful blouse. And he cried the truth until there was nothing left to cry and the most wonderful woman's most wonderful blouse was drenched in truth, and his eyes heaved dry until they heaved dry the most wonderful woman's blouse, and until he was a dried wrinkled balloon with no hope to ever reinflate.

The most wonderful woman rocked him back and forth, his eyes heaved dry, then dust, his eyes heaved dry dust, and then lawn clippings, his eyes heaved dry lawn clippings, then dust again, then nothing but the quietest whimper that the world had ever heard. Lips chapped, knees scabbed with eczema, toe nails cracked and plied, Henry looked up at the most wonderful woman, and she back to him. He talked while his long eyelashes that waved like feathers in outer space where there was no gravity at all.

"Where is Leaf?" he asked.

She spoke back from behind a tune that she hummed as she continued to rock back and forth. "Here sits the Lord Mayor, here sits his two men." His forehead, his two eyes.

"Is he okay?"

"Here sits the cock, here sits the hen." His left

cheek, cross to his right cheek.

"What's happened to him?"

"Here the little chickens, here they run in." His nose, his chapped lips.

"Why won't you answer me?" His long lashes waved.

"Chin-chopper, chin-chopper, chin-chopper, chin." All fingers under his chin, tickling. He couldn't help but smile and try to brush away the tickles, but then he covered it all with a scowl. A scar from the scowl remained, and he was too tired to ask again.

Henry stopped asking, and the most wonderful woman had lay him down in bed, the wrinkled balloon, vacuum sealed, scarred with scowl. She kissed his forehead, but he resisted.

She said, "You can't let things just pass," as she plucked the tips of his toes in twos. "Good night, my prince." And she left him, alone and in need of her support. She made him need her, needed her for her hope for him, which was as big as a tree trunk, which filled the sky with its branches. She hoped him the most wonderful things in the whole world, and he with none of his own hope.

But when the lights went out and the steps down the hallway had faded, Henry opened his hand, where he'd kept a little truth for himself. He cracked the shell of that truth and poured the one drop of hope that rested inside back into his eye, and it was a drop in a desert, but it was a start.

Leaf would not have saved a drop, and Henry

knew this. Leaf would have been unable to resist that *chin-chopper, chin-chopper, chin-chopper chin* and unable to retain that drop and pour it back into his desert eye. He would have given that too, and would have said he was just being nice, just helping the most wonderful woman feel useful, and he would have needed her hope, would have been addicted to it. But Henry saved a drop. It was not easy, but he'd done it once before and it was a tiny bit easier this time around.

This one drop he brought with him across the Running River and past the Stadium, and he flew with it up to the Queen Lizard's daughter's window. As he looked in the window and watched the daughter braid her hair into the three which she often wore, he felt ashamed. She had warned him about the most wonderful woman, told him what to do if he was ever caught and forced to tell truth. *Let the truth run free*, she whispered. *Let the truth run free and keep nothing for yourself. Come to me, and I will give you what you've lost. I WILL GIVE YOU WHAT YOU'VE LOST!* She roared with a smile that always blew the bangs out of Henry's face, and her breath perfumed of raspberries and the sweat from a cold glass of water. *And you will have more.*

Henry had panicked though, kept one for himself, and now he was ashamed. He walked home with his one drop. He found an old army chest in the alley behind the Stadium, and he put his one drop of hope in it. He put the chest in his closet, and he tried survive on just that one drop. He was further from Leaf than he'd ever been, and this was his sacrifice. But time is circular, so he would play it again and again, and he didn't see the Queen Lizard's daughter for seven years, until she interrupted the detrimental cycle, an interruption carefully orchestrated by the Queen Lizard herself. Henry started to remember her daughter, started seeing her in the periphery of his eye and etched her curves out of white paper and a pencil, and connected that with curves of awakedness.

Leaf held the etching before him and understood the confession, understood the conceit, and he admired his brother Henry for it. There would be no more distance between them.

CHAPTER 11
Leaving of Dry Heavings

I awoke to an empty bed, cluck hollow. Christine had gone to work and let me sleep. She worked as a designer at a photography studio. Her coworkers were older than she; she looked up to them. The disparity between us was bigger than that though. *I scared her*, she once said, sometimes she didn't know where I'd gone, lying next to her. I picked my shirt off the floor and stepped over the gate that kept Murray from sleeping with his surrogate mother. He was lying on the rug on the other side and barely lifted his head when I stepped over him. It was me for whom she bought the gate. I didn't like to sleep with the dog. I didn't want to share her. I found my shoes in front of the couch and put them on.

He looked up at me from under his bushy brow. I felt drained, bone dry. It was as if the extrication of the final chapter had quieted all of the aspects I'd spent so much time rabble rousing. It was as if they'd all lined up. There was no AJua, no Nobody. *The Heroin of the Nobilities in the Danger Zone* did not tell me to open the gate for Murray because it was the right thing to do, I did it out of weariness. He hopped to his feet, like a little lamb, and scampered to the bed, jumping up and settling down in front of the window, looking back at me. I did not want to fight him anymore; I did not have the energy for it. When I left I was so hungry. I rode on dirt bike tires with worn down treads.

So low in the flesh, so high in the bone, bone stricken with the part of me that was marked for the sacrifice, the part of me that I continually allowed to be sacrificed, the part of me I offered up to the false divinity that was also part of me. Those furtive polyhedral shapes that I saw when I had a fever as a child, *the offering*, I thought, and the pride in that offering, and then there was a projection of my brother too, seen only by me, sitting on the edge of my mother's bed, inexplicably linked to that offering. It was a liminal state, a mixture of the two worlds, the waking and the sleeping, and that was sacred, but it was not to be coveted under the rapture of a selfish child. It was a joy that should have been employed, and shared, for the understanding, for the connection and the company. I lost my job at the ice cream shop. They could tell with one look what was so hard for me to learn: I was under-employed.

I moved back into the city that fall and got a place by myself, not far from my brother. I was still very hungry. It became a full time job to organize all this new information. In order to continue to put shape to the complex systems that had been revealed, I needed conditioning. I needed energy to keep my focus, to keep everything in line. I began to eat fervently, consistently, with ritual, because I knew I forgot to do that. I ate when I wasn't hungry, which was most times. I ate oatmeal every morning, minutes after I awoke. I stuffed my face at lunch, heaping turkey sandwiches and turkey sandwiches. I preconceived meals, knowing exactly what dinner I would cook when I got home, knowing what dinners I would cook for the next week. I baked bread, tracked down recipes, saved leftover red beans and rice for a fast snack. I ate with my brother. I ate with my sisters in Chicago. I ate with my sisters not in Chicago. I ate with my mother and my father. I ate with my old friends, and I ate with my new friends. Mary called me up one day for the first time in years and we ate casserole over the phone.

I stopped trying to cut *SV of the EP* off of my bones, instead I fed him 'til he was strong and healthy. And now that I had everyone sitting at the same table, of the same mind, I had to feed them all. I had to work to feed them all because they ate so much. I put in the hours. I woke up early, and it was hard, but it got easier, and I began to enjoy it, and feel good about it. And you, you were there too.

You came and sat down with all of us one evening for a beautiful feast that *the Fool of the Uncanny in the World of Intimate Others* had put together. That boy cooked the best chicken casserole and mashed potatoes, just like my mother made 'em.

A year had gone by and my faculties were returning, my mindfulness, and most of all, my meat. You sat next to *the Heroin of the Nobilities in the Danger Zone*, whose fortitude you had very much come to respect, and I sat next to *SV of the EP* because I liked to watch over him myself, just to make sure he ate, and so he didn't slip away from us. We were whole now. *The Boy William of the Manboys in the Woods* was regaling us with a wonderful tale involving *the Muse of the Stars in the World of Childhood*, a piece of twine, and the stray cat that frequented the premises. Out of nowhere t*he Hero of the Curious in the Everyday World* wheeled an elderly in from off the kitchen. At first I thought that it was the *Old Person of the Greatests in the Playground*, but then I saw him watching the Sox game in his lounge chair.

"I was out in the garden, examining ladybugs, and look who I found wandering the grounds." Everyone stopped what they were doing when they realized what was happening. *The Dreamer of the Olympians in the Shadow World* started to well up in anticipation, and I thought, *what is going on here?* You looked to AJua, who was just as astonished as you were, and as she lifted her head, you saw the glazed eyes and toothless smile of the woman who'd died too many times to still be alive and in our dining room. *The Philosopher of the Daydreamers in the Everyday World* stated the obvious, but someone had to say it, because I was having trouble holding my head up, let alone speaking, "You must be *the Witch of the Charmers in the Hospital*."

She smiled and smacked her gums, "Eh, who made them mashed potatoes, smell just like your mother's." No one said a word, then laughter and applause broke the astonishment. *Hero of the Curious* wheeled her right in between you and me, because he knew how important this was to us. I scooted over and made room while *Fool of the Uncanny* scooped her a big plate of mashed potatoes and chicken casserole. You cut her a slice of hot bread, and *the Sacrificial Victim of the*

Earthy People gave up his glass of wine so that she could properly imbibe. I was so touched by his gesture that I put my hand over his to show him. He waited patiently until I was done and then went to fetch himself another glass. She leaned over and kissed you on the side of your head, and I let a few tears escape, but it was not the gushing kind.

She whispered, "I knew there was more," and you couldn't even think of the words to thank her.

"For a while I thought that might be it for me," You whispered back.

She just repeated, "I knew there was more," and took a bite of her mashed potatoes.

The Boy William spoke up, I thought to give a toast, but instead said, like my father always said, "Shall we pray." We all held hands, and it still came out as one word:

B l e s s u s O L o r d f o r t h e s e t h y g i f t s w h i c h w e a r e a b o u t t o r e c e i v e t h r o u g h y o u r b o u n t y t h r o u g h C h r i s t o u r L o r d A m e n 'N a m e o f t h e F a t h e r t h e S o n a n d H o l y S p i r i t A m e n.

"And thank you for bringing *the Witch of the Charmers in the Hospital* back to us. And Bless Nobody," I said, "which of course I don't mean that I don't want anyone to be blessed, but that I want Nobody, who could not be here with us tonight, because he exists only in AJua's head, to be blessed. Thank you. Amen." AJua smiled and crossed himself as I stumbled through the identification of a being who was inherently so hard to identify, and nodded his head when I finished.

"Let's eat!" said *the Boy William*, and everyone dug in. I noticed the color had returned to *the Witch's* cheeks as her head danced back and forth between spoonfuls, and she was suspiciously vibrant, something that she instantly downplayed when she saw me taking note. "I am but part of you," she said with a light smile and sleepy eyes, "You're getting much too old to fool yourself." I appreciated her candor.

The End

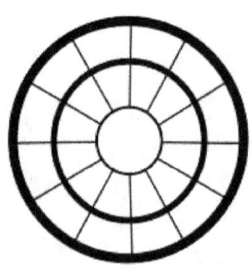

Published by
Little Man

Thanks for being patient, Anne.